Further Titles by Lucilla

ENDE

HOSPITA

MARSH BLOOD

MARSH BLOOD

Lucilla Andrews

This edition published in Great Britain 1993 by
SEVERN HOUSE PUBLISHERS LTD of
9–15 High Street, Sutton, Surrey SM1 1DF.
Originally published in Great Britain in 1980 under the
pseudonym of Joanna Marcus by Hutchinson & Co. Ltd.

British Library Cataloguing in Publication Data
Andrews, Lucilla
  Marsh Blood. – New ed
  I. Title
  823.914 [F]

  ISBN 0-7278-4563-2

Typeset by Hewer Text Composition Services, Edinburgh.
Printed and bound in Great Britain by
Redwood Books, Trowbridge, Wiltshire.

I

I sensed that I was *persona non grata* immediately I walked into the oak-panelled reception hall that afternoon and it wasn't only because I wasn't carrying a gun. It was over three years since I'd last had that sensation but in my brief marriage I'd experienced it often enough when meeting my late husband's old friends and new creditors to recognize it instantly. That no one had ever given Charles credit twice was amongst the reasons why I seldom used his surname and the couple who owned and ran Harbour Inn hadn't recognized it on the reservation my Mr Smith made for me last week when I was down with flu.

Mr Smith was my elderly solicitor. Sue Denver, his daughter, and her husband, Francis, had just driven across the marsh with me. We'd come in convoy: Francis had driven me in his Audi; Sue had followed in my Allegro. They had not seen me in, as Sue couldn't keep mummy waiting. (On this occasion his name was Gordon.) 'You don't mind, Rose darling,' she drawled, 'but I did promise mummy I'd be at Cliffhill Town Hall by three, it's another thirty-three miles and it's useless saying Francis'll make it easily. What's the good of a fast car on a road that twists every few yards?' She hauled on a floppy-brimmed suede hat to protect her gold head from the thin rain and leapt into the passenger seat of the Audi before Francis had deposited my suitcase and sketching haversack in the reception hall. 'Darling, do come on! Rose'll be fine and anyway I'm seeing

5

her at mummy's exhibition tomorrow afternoon and she can tell me then if it's all too hideous. Don't forget, Rose – the opening's at two – byeee!'

Francis removed his tweed cap, smoothed his dark-red hair and looked perturbed. 'I wish we didn't have to rush away, Rose. If you don't like it here just give us a ring and I'll come and collect you. Take it easy – sure you don't mind our vanishing like this?'

'Of course not. Thanks a lot for bringing me over.'

He had a delightful smile. 'You always understand. See you. Coming, Susie – ' He hurried off.

I understood Sue, if not always Francis, possibly as I saw so much less of him. His job as a consultant mining engineer regularly took him abroad for months at a time. Sue was her parents' only child and had been born when they had about given up hope of having a family. It remained her mother's pride that she had never been able to deny her daughter anything. Her father still treated her as if she were nine years old. At twenty-nine she was a tall sexy blonde with a lovely figure and after four years' marriage Francis continued to give the impression that for him the honeymoon hadn't ended. Of course, he was away so much. They lived just outside St Martin's village, were my nearest neighbours and, as Sue never failed to inform strangers she considered socially acceptable, my greatest friends. That Sue and I knew she wouldn't have bought a flag on her doorstep from me, had I not owned more good farming land than anyone else on our part of the marsh, worried neither of us. Sue never bothered what other women thought of her and I was a realist. For the first twenty-three years of my life I'd been poor; for the last three, rich. As has been said, rich was better.

The owner-managers of Harbour Inn were a Mr and Mrs Evans-Williams. They surveyed me with the expressions the middle-aged, middle-class English reserve for those who threaten the established order. They were of the generation that regarded an unaccompanied young woman booking in at an English hotel as still in that category. I was rather sorry I'd never got round to buying a mink. Then they could've been sure I was on the game.

'Just complete this form, please,' Mrs Evans-Williams requested in well-modulated tones, flicking it across the carved black oak reception counter. She was a tallish thin woman with blue hair, slightly protruding grey eyes, a tight mouth and rows of beads. 'When Mr Smith of Smith, Smith and Smith of Astead telephoned to cancel our previous booking for room five – double room with private bath – and thereupon booked it for your sole use for one week from this day, he merely gave us your name on that occasion, and in his letter of confirmation. Are we to understand your address remains care of his office?'

Being *persona non grata* I forbore to explain that Mr Smith's ingrained objection to handing out gratuitous information to strangers included the weather. 'No.' I began on the form.

Mr Evans-Williams tugged his neat moustache disapprovingly. He was a neat, straight-backed, grey little man with a military haircut, and the hot, angry eyes of a hard drinker. But from the steadiness of his hands he knew when to pocket the cellar keys. 'Afraid you may find us rather dull, Mrs . . . Er as you don't shoot. Height of the season. Best wild-duck shooting in the country on Harbour Marsh. We've only the five double rooms – no room for more and frankly we aren't sorry. We like the small homely atmosphere and it seems to suit our guests. Our present eight all came together last year and the year before. Keen as mustard and cracking good shots – the two ladies included. But as they're up early they like early nights so we don't encourage non-residents in the shooting season. Need your sleep if you're out after duck from dawn till dusk.'

I returned the form. 'Surely you only get duck at dawn and dusk when the flights come in. What do they go after in the intervals? Snipe?'

'Know something of the marsh, eh?' He glanced at the form and his wife did the same over his shoulder. I knew from their faces what was coming. It came. After three years it still had me torn between the desires to shout with laughter and throw up.

'Oh, dear, we do apologize!' Mrs Evans-Williams clutched her beads and had she possessed a bosom would have flung it out in welcome. 'I'm afraid we just didn't recognize your married name. We've always thought of you – the whole marsh thinks of you – as Rose Endel of Endel. And that beautiful old house! Tragic! Tragic! We'd just bought this place three years ago when we heard – the whole marsh heard – how that lovely old roof had fallen in and killed poor young Mr Endel and his dear wife and her young brother and so nearly killed you – the last of the Endels. The last of that fine old marsh family – just a girl – a newly widowed girl with all that responsibility on her young shoulders. We were so distressed for you – remember how distressed we were, Johnnie?'

Johnnie remembered and grunted to prove it.

'And you've come to us for a little holiday? Had flu? Come to rest in Harbour?' Her cup was running over. 'Naturally one understands why Mr Smith had to be careful. Solicitors are always so discreet and with such a young and charming client he won't want to risk encouraging fortune hunters.'

Johnnie Evans-Williams had recovered. 'No chance of that here, ma'am. Just duck hunters, eh? But we mustn't keep you standing around if you've been under the weather.

Give young Trevor a shout, Helen, and we'll take this good lady to her room – or would you first care for a quick look round our humble hostelry, ma'am? Only this floor and one upper. You would? Splendid! Afraid it won't be the scale you're accustomed to.'

'Endel's not exactly Blenheim, Mr Evans-Williams.'

From his shrug the only difference lay in the fact that Sir Winston Churchill had not been born in Endel House. 'Much older than Blenheim, surely?'

'Only a couple of centuries.' I looked around. 'I should say more or less the same age as this place.'

Mrs Evans-Williams giggled girlishly. 'That's what I love about you marshfolk. You talk of hundreds of years back as if it were yesterday.'

Her husband grinned boyishly. 'Very right and proper. Continuity and stability – those are the things that matter, eh?'

Something about him struck a mental chord I couldn't place and had no time to pursue as a fair-haired youth in a porter's waistcoat had appeared through the swing door at the back of the hall. 'Nip these bags up to five for madam, Trevor, then nip back and keep an eye here. Not,' Mr Evans-Williams added to me, 'that we're likely to have any visitors this far off the map this afternoon. Bar's just closing. We don't do non-resident teas in the shooting season. Different in summer. Can't see the marsh for visitors. Same your way, I expect. Just step this way, ma'am, and I trust you'll approve our attempts to haul the old lady into the second half of the twentieth century without too much damaging her ancient charms.'

Harbour Inn had been an inn on and off for some 400-odd years. In the off periods it had housed boats, nets, fishing tackle, fodder, sheep, chickens, fishermen, smugglers – on the rare occasions when the two occupations were not synonymous – musketeers waiting for Napoleon, and machine-gun crews waiting for Hitler. It was a low, sturdy, L-shaped little building that stood on a natural mound that was divided by a dyke from the solitary, narrow, built-up road that wound between dykes and over dyke bridges from the main coast road running along by the sea wall, to Harbour village three miles inland. The inn and its outhouses across the flagged yard were the only habitable buildings between the village that was due west, and the sea that was half a mile off due east, and four miles off north and south. The sea beyond the solid high concrete wall that edged the entire marsh coast was only visible from the upper windows of the inn as all the surrounding land was below sea-level. The sound of the sea was as constant as the salt in the clean marsh air and only on the calmest day was there no angry growl of the forbidden sea lashing the wall at high water.

There were no crops on Harbour Marsh. The soil was too salty. From autumn to late spring there were no sheep as the land was too often flooded. The flat fields were lacerated by the deep dykes up which the sea ran at spring tides and pointed hungry green fingers at the inn. That land had been the tranquil home for thousands of birds, a resting place for migrants and a bird-watchers' paradise, until the guns arrived. The Evans-Williamses, possibly because they were incomers, had had the acumen to recognize the inn's potential for duck hunters and, when they bought it, acquired the local shooting rights. According to local gossip, and as I now saw for myself, they had transformed, with the kind of impeccable taste that costs a great deal of money, what had degenerated into a run-down bed-and-breakfast boozer into one of the most comfortable and exclusive private sporting hotels on the south-east coast.

When first built, the inn had stood on one arm of a small, natural, prosperous fishing harbour and catered for travellers on the cross-Channel packets. It had been about forty years old when one of the week-long storms that had ravaged that part of the English coast at varying intervals while the Plantagenets and Tudors occupied the throne had flung up enough silt, pebbles and sand to ruin the harbour permanently, and leave a new high-water line half a mile further out than the old. The fisherfolk had waited for a few more years in the hope that another storm would return their lost harbour. Eventually they lost patience and brick by brick, removed their church and homes three miles inland, on to land that when drained would be more suitable for crops and grazing. The then incumbent innkeeper had refused to move, so they left him and his inn. On their new site they dug more dykes, built a high mound for their church, smaller mounds for their homes, and rebuilt their bricks. They named their village Harbour, the isthmus Harbour Marsh and the new stretch they added to the sea wall, the Harbour Wall. This last still confused visiting foreigners who expected to find a harbour on the other side. 'Foreigners' in this context covered all nationalities including the English born on the mainland fifty miles inland who had not at least one marsh-born parent.

'Geography clear, ma'am? Residents only off this side of the hall. Lounge, television room, gun room, and residents' public telephones through that last door. We've put a public box for non-residents between the bar and dining room over the other side and raised a door or two there. We didn't want to spoil these so we've let 'em be and shoved up notices warning all over five foot nine to mind their heads. Not that you have to worry, eh?'

'No, indeed,' cooed Mrs Evans-Williams. 'So petite! Such a typical black-haired, black-eyed little marshwoman!'

'We're also reputed to have yellow bellies and webbed feet.'

They must have heard that *ad nauseam*. It didn't dim their joy. 'How about the cellars? Care to take a look at the special cold store we've had put in to take the bags?'

'Thanks, but no. I'm not all that keen on looking at dead birds.'

Their renewed guffaws reminded me of something Mr Smith once said, 'It is a strange fact of life, my dear Rose, that people seldom believe the truth when they hear it.'

A new natural-pine staircase ran up from the hall to the guest rooms on the first floor. A very narrow, uneven-floored passage covered by a thick, dark-blue wall-to-wall bisected the two double rooms that lay off either side of the long arm of the L, and had new fire doors at both ends. Johnnie said, 'We've left in the old twisting stairs that run up to the attics. God forbid you should need to know this, but if you should – just through those doors at the far end. Young Trevor, our cook, and his missus have rooms in the attics, the rest of our staff come out daily from Harbour. Through here' – he opened the fire doors at the angle of the L 'five on your left, six right. Six we call Johnnie's suite. Johnnie being your humble servant.' He opened the door of a neat, small, plainly furnished single room with a minute bathroom visible through an open door beyond. 'I use this when we've a full house – as now. Only fair to our guests to have one of us on tap at night. We've our own snug little billet over the garages. And this' – he bowed me into room 5 – 'yours, ma'am. We trust it suits.'

I looked around the clean, warm, attractively furnished double room and smiled. 'Admirably, thanks. How lovely. No phone and no telly.'

'May lose us the odd stars but never lost us a customer yet. Come to Harbour Inn and discover lost civilization, that's our motto,' declared Johnnie. 'Nothing to offer but good food, good beds, clean air, quiet, splendid views and splendid shooting.' He noticed my haversack. 'Got an easel in there?'

'Yes.' I walked over to the only one of the low, leaded windows that directly overlooked the marsh to conceal my reaction to his including shooting in his idea of civilization. The two others overlooked the yard. I watched a black and white cloud of lapwing settle on the greenish-grey land. 'I like drawing birds and I've heard you've still a greater variety here than we have on Midstreet Marsh.' Their silence made me look round. 'Don't worry about my getting in your guns' light. I'll check with you first where it's safe to go.'

Mrs Evans-Williams twisted her beads and her husband tugged at his moustache. 'Be grateful if you would,' he admitted. 'Can't be too careful when the guns are out and – well – frankly – problem is, we're having a bit of poacher trouble *pro tem.* Not surprising. Bound to happen when incomers lease the rights over land the locals have regarded as their birthright for centuries. You get this trouble?'

'Not really,' was all I said. There was no need to explain that I didn't lease my shooting rights or use them myself, but left them by unspoken agreement with my farm manager, Walt Ames. Walt was a very reliable and tough local man, who respected without sharing my anti-blood-sports view, and on the side allowed his farm workers, relations, friends and neighbours to shoot for their own consumption and to keep the stock in hand, but not for sale.

My views here had made my response to Mr Smith's suggestion for this week one of horror. But my GP had ganged up with him and together they had reminded me they had known my late father as a boy, of their responsibilities for my welfare, of my lack of protective relatives, of the sleep they would lose and the sorrow it would occasion their wives if I failed to take their advice. Not feeling strong enough to stay in the fight, I'd given in and comforted myself with the reflection that at least coming to Harbour would save me from having to use more energy than was necessary for slinging a few clothes in a suitcase and driving over.

In the event I hadn't to do either for myself. Sue Denver had insisted on organizing my departure and packing. 'Francis must drive you and I'll bring yours. Don't worry about that, as my Allegro's your twin.'

'If you bring mine, how'll you get home from Cliffhill? Francis won't want to spend the afternoon helping the Art Society set up its exhibition.'

'Darling, don't be thick! You know Francis loathes arty-crafties and anyway the poor darling's got a business date in Astead at four. Mummy's bossing the show as she's this year's Chairman of the Organizing Committee. She'll run me home or – um – if she's too hectically busy I'll cadge a lift off Gordon. He'll have to hire a van. He can't cart his pictures around on his motorbike. I don't suppose he'll mind.'

'Gordon?' At the moment the name meant nothing to my cotton-wool brain. 'For God's sake, Sue, which one's Gordon?'

'You must remember! You met him at last year's show. That Scotch painter who lives in Cliffhill – the real painter – rather gorgeous in an uncouth sort of way. Black beard and most dreamy eyes – and don't look like that, Rose! You know very well Francis never minds my having my own friends – so why should you? Now! What clothes do you want to take on your hols?'

I looked at my unpacked suitcase while Johnnie continued his anxious spiel on the dangers of poachers. The prospect of tomorrow's annual 'do' of the Cliffhill Art Society, worried me far more than the thought of my accidentally collecting a load of shot. 'I'll be careful,' I promised, 'though, to be honest, I don't think I'll be in much danger. I doubt I'll go out of sight of this inn and I imagine from some window here you can overlook the whole isthmus. The last thing any poacher wants to do is advertise his or her presence and, from all I've heard, they only pop up once the light's begun to fade. I won't be out sketching at dawn or dusk. But thanks for giving me the picture.'

'Cards on the table, that's our motto!'

'Always.' Mrs Evans-Williams let go of her beads. 'Now how about a nice pot of tea? Up here? Or in the lounge by that lovely log fire?'

I took the hint. My room was pleasantly warm, but I preferred logs to central heating and from what they had said I should have the lounge to myself for a few more hours. I said I'd be down once I'd unpacked, they removed themselves and I spent a minute or so looking at the closed door and wondering why flu left one feeling so suicidal once it was over. Perhaps the old boys were right. This was my first break in over two and a half years. It would be soothing to sit and stare for a week. There was never time for either at Endel now that I did all the bookwork for the farm and the rest of the estate; and for most of the year the rebuilt house was filled with disabled children and their attendants on what, for the children, was a country holiday by the sea.

A glint of white drew me to the marsh window. I went over and watched a white car turn off the sea road and up towards the inn. I couldn't see the solitary driver clearly but from the care with which he was negotiating the turns and low-walled humped stone bridges, he was aware of the deceptive innocence of the gentle orange reed-mace sticking up above the quiet brown water. All those dykes could swallow a lorry and hold it down in the deadly reedy slime. He slowed to crawl over the final bridge on to the few yards of cinder road that ran down into the yard. I had moved away and glanced incuriously out of one of the front windows when the driver got out, flexing his wide shoulders as if he had been driving too long. I stiffened as if I'd had an electric shock.

The very fair-headed man in his mid-thirties below didn't notice me at the window. He looked around with the bemused expression of someone wondering if he'd come to the right place. I knew he had and I knew his name. David Lofthouse. What I didn't know was why he wasn't in Australia. He was a physicist and had gone out there to work on some project for his firm the day following our farewell dinner in London on the last evening of my last break.

Outwardly, he hadn't altered much. His hair was more bleached and his square face had a colour-supplement tan, but he still wore the same-shaped black-rimmed glasses and still hitched them down to look over the tops when he wanted a better look at a close object. He was studying the inn sign roughly four feet below when I opened my window. He glanced up and for several seconds we looked at each other in the same guarded way and then, slowly, we both smiled.

He raised a hand. 'Hi, Rose! Just passing.' He still used the short northern 'a'.

'Hi, David. Birmingham by way of Beachy Head?'

'Yep. Thought I'd stop by and buy you a drink.'

'You've been in the colonies too long, chum. Welcome back to Britain's licensing laws. Bar's closed.'

'Oh, God. I'm not stopping.'

'Hang about before you take off for another couple of years. How did you know I was here? Why didn't you tell me you were coming back? When did you get back?'

'Six hours back.' He turned up the collar of his tweed overcoat. 'I drove straight from Gatwick to Endel like I said on my postcard –'

'I never got that one –'

'That's what your manager bloke Walt Ames said. "If she'd had it, Mr Lofthouse" ' – he mimicked Walt's gentle,

16

broad-vowelled voice very well – ' "she'd not have gone off leaving an old friend to find the door closed." He said,' he went on in his own deep North-Country voice, 'you'd just left for here with some neighbours.'

'Sue and Francis Denver. I expect you remember them – '

'Can't remember if I do or not, though I did old Ames. Way back we supped more than the odd jar at the Crown in St Martin's. He said why didn't I follow on, so here I am. Are you going to come down or do I have to climb up? And if I do, I'll tell you straight I've forgotten me bloody guitar, I've no bloody head for heights and, what's more,' he added reproachfully, 'I'm bloody freezing to death.'

I laughed. 'Freezing? A Yorkshireman on a nice November day in the soft South? It's even stopped raining. This'll teach you to take off for the outback. Go on in and tell them – ' but Johnnie had bustled out below. I explained the situation. 'I presume Mr Lofthouse can be my guest for tea in the lounge?'

'Naturally, ma'am. Any friend of yours, more than welcome.' He offered his hand to David. 'Johnnie Evans-Williams. Mine host of this humble hostelry. Come on in, sir – car locked? Wise chap! Not necessary here, I'm thankful to say, but better safe than sorry, eh? Watch your head on that door and all the doors, Mr Lofthouse. Big sturdy chap like you could do yourself a nasty mischief if you're not careful!'

I sat at the dressing-table intending to re-do my hair and face and instead gazed at my reflection. I didn't see it. I saw a face David had never seen but glimpsed every time he shaved. And then other men's faces, Endel faces, with my own colouring and bone-structure. All the Endels had dark eyes and first names that began with 'R'; all the Endels had Endel blood. Fine old blood; some of the finest blood in England. Everyone said so. Only two people, David Lofthouse and myself, knew that in the last three generations three Endel men had died undetected murderers. My grandfather had tried to murder my father, his younger son, and succeeded in murdering David's uncle; his eldest son had been an accessary to both facts; his only grandson, my cousin Robert, had tried to murder me a few hours before he murdered his brother-in-law and the roof of Endel buried his body and the secret of his illegitimacy. David and I alone had known the truth and, since I was then the only living legal heir, there had been no point in saying this had been the case since my grandfather's death, as both his sons had been killed in the last war. Endel was entailed and could only be inherited by the legitimate children of born Endels. It would have gone to the crown three years ago had David not risked his life to save mine.

My friends knew he had saved my life, knew he had gone to Australia, and were convinced he was why I was still a widow. Several, from time to time, and especially Sue Denver, lectured me sternly, 'If you won't think of yourself, think of poor David having to go off big-game hunting abos or whatever and think of Endel. If you don't remarry and have kids, the entail and family will die out with you. I can't imagine why you won't write and ask him to come back. Everyone knew he was absolutely sold on you. . . .'

Walt Ames was a quiet man and, in common with most quiet men, a great talker. Ten minutes after he dropped in for his nightly pint at the Crown this evening, every friend or foe I possessed would either be drinking David's and my health or reaching for the hemlock. Even the foes, if they suspected, had never dared hint about my late relatives' nasty habits. The Endels had always known how to keep their own and other mouths shut. So did I. Strong stuff that Endel blood, I decided, and grimaced. Then I did my hair carefully and put on some lipstick.

Johnnie was just leaving the lounge. 'Tea along in two shakes of a lamb's tail.' He closed the door on David and myself.

The lounge faced north and at this time of the year needed artificial light all day. There were no overhead lights. The small lamps fixed to the dark-panelled walls and the larger reading lamps on the coffee tables all had dark-yellow shades that threw golden pools on to the bronze leather armchairs and sofas and thick brown carpet. The low black ceiling beams and the cases of dead stuffed birds that lined the walls were in shadow; the flickering logs filled the room with more and moving shadows; none was as tangible as the shadows we had brought in with us.

He was standing by the fire still in his overcoat and threw away a half-smoked cigarette. 'It's not often one's fantasies fall short of reality,' he remarked conversationally. 'You're even better to look at now than you were.' He came over, removed his glasses and kissed me. That hadn't changed either. He always kissed very well. 'If you've decided to wed me,' he said 'feel free to ask.'

I put my hands on his shoulders. 'I still have the option?'

'Oh, aye.' He replaced his glasses. 'Well?'

'Sorry. Once was enough.'

'Hell, love, you don't have to make an honest bloke of me. I'm not fussy. Just bloody frustrated.'

I smiled. 'Two and a half years unbroken celibacy in the Antipodes, of course.'

His grin exposed his very good teeth. 'I'd to remember company rules. British Chemicals Consolidated get hellish nasty with employees who neglect their general health.'

'For God's sake, man, why didn't you marry one?'

'I've this problem. Allergic to white gloves.'

'To – what?'

'White gloves. And putting on hats for stepping out to

the shops. And all those lovely bronzed sexless bodies and all those hearty outdoor sports. Where's me weedy, white, decadent Pom Sheila who only fancies the one indoor sport same as me, I cried – piteously. And got the first flight out soon as BCC let me off the hook. So once is still enough?'

'Sorry. Yes. But I'm delighted to see you.'

'That's good.' He kissed me again. 'Remember when one look at your late's doppelgänger and you all but ran screaming? We progress.' He moved away and lit a cigarette. 'If I vanish a couple more years, when I next show up you might even kiss me back. Ten years from now you'll be asking me to have you – and it won't have to be nicely.'

I sat on the sofa. 'I'll bear that in mind.'

'You do that.' He sat by me. 'Too bad I can't twist your arm. You're the only loaded bird I know. How else can I lay my hands on all that lovely lolly?'

I could've told him. My Mr Smith didn't think that a good idea. 'Tell me about the postcard I should've had and why nothing but postcards even at Christmas?'

'I am,' he said with dignity, 'public-spirited. Why deny the St Martin's post office and the neighbours the pleasure of knowing I hope this finds you as it leaves me which is in the pink with the nasty upset stomach quite settled? Or of knowing the wandering lad was still hoping? Best way I knew of keeping tabs. If you'd wed again and forgotten to tell me, half your neighbours would have sent me joyful cables with the bad news. This card you've not had I posted the day I flew from Brisbane. It said BCC were arranging to have my new car waiting at Gatwick, that I'd come straight to Endel and hope to cadge a bed there for tonight and maybe a few more. I don't have to show up at the Coventry office till next week. You'd said on the card you'd a spare room in the flat you've made for yourself on the ground floor of the old homestead.' He paused. 'I see you've used most of the old bricks and tiles.'

'They were there. How – how do you feel? Seeing the house back up on its mound?'

He looked into the fire. 'Like a ghost from my own past – till I heard the kids laughing.' He faced me. 'Walt Ames held open the front door for me to see them playing chuck-the-bean-bag in the hall. Their wheelchairs weren't doing a lot for the floor polish but their presence was doing one hell of a lot for the atmosphere. What gave you the notion to lend it out to these kids' societies?'

I needed time. He didn't hurry me. 'You'd been gone about a month when the insurance assessors finally settled the figure. It wasn't the full amount as so much of the house was still repairable, but quite enough to rebuild all that had come down. The farm was doing well, other rents coming in and – and all mine.' I looked at him. 'David, I felt so guilty. I'd done nothing to earn any of it. Just by sheer chance I happened to be born my father's only child.'

'And from what Walt said, most of those poor kids just chanced to be born disabled and, as you're not allowed to sell or give it away because of the entail, you lend the joint.'

I was grateful for his quick comprehension. It was impossible to remember that once this had frightened me. 'That's right.'

'That took guts, love.' He reached for my hand. 'Why didn't you write me about the kids?'

'Not enough room on a postcard.'

'That's for sure. But you should've got the one from Brisbane. Posted it myself over three weeks ago.'

'You've not taken that time to fly back?'

'No. BCC wanted me in West Germany first, then Paris. I flew over from France this morning. So it's got held up or lost in the post. So what else is new in beautiful broken-down

Britain? Tell me all. For starters' – he stood up to remove his coat, then sat down again – 'tell me what you're doing in this ornithological mausoleum. You used to be anti-blood-sports. Why come here for a rest cure?'

The fair-haired Trevor had come in with our tea. I waited till we were alone to explain. 'I wish,' I added, 'I'd had your card. We could've stayed at Endel.'

'Let's work on that later. Old Smith? Tall, gaunt old boy with white hair and face like a wet Monday in Wigan?'

'I've never been to Wigan, but – yes. Sue Denver's father. Remember the Denvers now? They've got that lovely converted Elizabethan farmhouse on the Endel side of St Martin's. The Smiths gave it them for a wedding present.'

He frowned, then grinned hugely. 'Blonde bird with legs and silent Pre-Raphaelite hubby on a string? Sure. I remember Hot Pants Susie.' He chuckled. 'If you didn't fancy me, time was when she just might've – but I didn't fancy hubby'd like it. He get his blue Jag. as a wedding present?'

'No! He earns good money doing whatever consultant mining engineers do in foreign parts. Got a red Audi now.'

'He's doing all right.' He looked around. 'So are they here from the look. Must cost a bomb to stay here. Not that you'll have to worry.'

I said quietly, 'No. Though there are many times when I still don't believe that.'

'I'll bet.' He looked at me over his glasses. 'How many blokes have offered you hand and heart for a share in the loot. Three figures?'

'Not quite.'

'Know something, love? I'm just thanking God for the late Charles D. and that's one pat on the back I never thought to hand the poor bastard. He rates it. If he hadn't bashed some sense into you by marrying you, you'd be a bloody sitting duck. Twenty-six, lovely and loaded. What more could any bloke ask.'

'You've never asked.'

'Nor will I.' He smiled into my eyes. 'I'll just simper coyly and let you seduce me.'

'Oh, I'm so sorry!' Mrs Evans-Williams fluttered in the doorway. 'There's a telephone call for Dr Lofthouse – at least the man said Doctor and I think he's from the BBC.'

'BCC.' David stood up. 'I'm not medically qualified.'

I said, 'He's a PhD, but modest. He doesn't like to advertise the computer between his ears.'

David scowled, she trilled joyously and ushered him out. I was rather relieved to have a breather. Seeing him again had disturbed me more than I cared. I looked around for some anodyne and found it framed on one wall.

It was a sixteenth-century map of the marsh drawn when the fishing harbour still existed at the bottom right corner. The inn was marked and so was the church. The names of the various areas of marsh that echoed the original Celtic inhabitants and Roman and Norse invaders were depicted in elegant Elizabethan lettering, and forty miles due north of the fishing harbour a tiny squashed box on a miniature hillock was labelled ENDELLE and encircled with HERE BE MIFTRETE MERSHE. Midstreet village was missing as already the sea had swept it away, and so was the Marsh Ditch that divided marsh from mainland, as it had not yet been dug. The low hills of the mainland were speckled with outsize sheep, with AFTEDE tersely topping their northern tip and HERE BE CLYFEHILLE surmounting the castellated boxes floating over the southern end. The sea ran from top to bottom and occupied one-third of the east side of the map. The sea was alive with wooden galleons with bulging sails, fishing boats with single sails; empty rowing boats that looked modern crowded every cove and dyke mouth; and giant fish jostled for space in the fishing grounds. The prevailing winds were blown through the pursed lips of fat flying cherubs; other cherubs perched on offshore rocks with down-pointed sea-spears to warn of the dangers to shipping; and all down the coastline trios of sea-serpents marked the shifting sands.

'Remarkably evil-looking serpents.' David was beside me. 'I don't remember hearing there were quicksands off Harbour.'

'I don't think there are now. I think the storm filled them. Was it BCC?'

'Yep. They got this number from Walt Ames. They only wanted to tell me I needn't show up for three weeks.' He peered more closely at the map. 'Only one thing missing. No here be dragons.'

My mind was elsewhere. I said vaguely, 'The Endels must've finished them off.'

He glanced at me. 'Uh-huh. Any more tea in that pot?'

We went back to the sofa. I refilled his cup and he told me he had just been asking Mrs Evans-Williams if she could recommend some place nearby where he could get a bed for tonight. 'I said you'd told me this place is full. She had a better idea. No, love – not your spare bed. She's not as daft as she looks. This is a respectable joint and that's the way she's keeping it. But she says hubby has a single room he uses and might let me have it for the night and she'll have a word soon as he gets in. He went out a while back to help bring in the day's bag. She says they'll all be in soon now the light's gone. I said fine, if she can swing it. That all right with you?'

'Sure. Fine.'

He gave me a long, thoughtful look. 'Stop sweating, Rose. You don't owe me anything.'

'Oh, no. Just my life and all I possess.'

'Balls. If you'd not lugged my unconscious body out of

24

Endel just before the roof gave, it would've been a quadruple, not triple funeral. It was your father who sired you, not me. So knock that bloody chip off and tell me something I don't know. Mrs Wassname-Wassname'll swing this. She doesn't fancy me but she fancies my custom. Why? If this joint's doing as well as it looks and you say, they don't need it.'

I had to wait until my adrenalin rate returned to normal. 'Maybe she thinks having you around will lessen the chances of my having my head blown off.'

'Christ,' he groaned, 'no! If someone else is out to murder you for your lolly, I'm off! I'm not going through that one again!'

I suddenly felt much happier. I laughed. 'Now you can stop sweating, chum.' I told him about the poachers, and then of my few minutes as *persona non grata.* 'And after, all was sweetness and light. Yeuk!'

He frowned. 'Can't have it all ways – but – seeing they know their business I'd have thought they checked up on you before you showed up.'

'How? They wouldn't get anything out of Mr Smith or his office. None of my friends has stayed here and the only one I know to have dropped in here occasionally is Francis and that's just for a drink. He's not the chatty type. If you were a woman you'd know there's nothing odd about their reception. Ask any woman who's ever walked alone into the dining room of any good British hotel.'

'I have heard that.' He paused. 'These poachers. Serious problem now?'

'No more than always. I think they're just fussing.'

'Wouldn't do their business any good locally if anything happened to you here. Not,' he added thoughtfully, 'that there's anyone left to want to rub you out. If you don't get yourself another husband and some kids, presumably either the crown or some charity collects. And you must've made a will. If old Smith knows his job he'll have had you tie the lot up tight.'

I studied my hands. 'He knows his job.'

'And has told you to keep your mouth shut?' I nodded. 'That's sense. Even if the cats' home gets the jackpot it's daft to advertise to whom you might be worth more dead than alive.'

'Much what he said and – ' I broke off as again the door opened.

Two young women, one a blonde, the other a brunette, and a large middle-aged man had piled in breathlessly congratulating themselves and each other on being handy with guns. As they were all talking simultaneously it was a few minutes before we realized what they were actually trying to tell us. Someone else, it seemed, was not quite so handy. Someone had just shot Johnnie Evans-Williams.

David and I exchanged the same glances as we got to our feet. He turned to the newcomers. 'Oh, aye? Manslaughter or murder?' he inquired politely.

2

'Sweetie, please don't chill our blood any more. He's only been winged,' wailed the brunette, in a South London twang. She was tallish and slender, even in bulky clothes, and had dramatic dark eyes, a wide sexual mouth and the kind of face that was vividly attractive or hard, depending on the owner's mood. She looked about twenty years younger than the large man whom she introduced as her husband. 'Renny le Vere. I'm Angie and this is Linda McCabe. Linda's husband Nick is a fabulous Canadian medic which is such a godsend as he's coping with poor Johnnie and otherwise we'd have to make a mercy dash to that old soak's surgery at Harbour.'

Renny le Vere looked badly in need of a drink and a seat but remained politely on his feet while I introduced David and myself. Linda McCabe was too shocked for civilities and flopped into an armchair. She was quite pretty and would have been more so had she not obviously cut her hair herself and neglected her pink and white complexion. Her face was reddened by the wind and her nose was peeling. Had we met elsewhere I would instantly have taped her as lower-income, higher-education. I was right about the last. She was an economics graduate who wrote intelligent pamphlets on the cost of living and the erudite captions for the Baby Bozo Books For Infants beloved by childless reviewers. They didn't sell well.

I said, 'So he's not badly hurt?'

'Thank God, sweetie, no. He caught the lot in the fleshy part of the back of his arm but it missed his shoulder. Nick says he can cope. Isn't it just too fabulous to have our own friendly neighbourhood physician in the party?'

Linda put in sulkily, 'Nick's a surgical registrar, Angie. You should know that by now.'

Angie le Vere flapped blackened eyelashes. 'Sweetie, you know me! I forget everything.'

Renny le Vere smiled wearily at his wife. Beneath the bags under his eyes, the heavy jowls and the bulging stomach were the visible remains of a good-looking man with clever, amused eyes. His Oxbridge voice was tired. 'Strange species, medics. Take our worthy Nick. He spends his entire working life chopping up humans and his free time killing God's harmless creatures.'

Linda rounded on him. 'You should talk! You've been shooting since before Nick and I were born.'

Renny raised a defensive hand. 'Don't kick a chap when he's down, dear girl. Don't I know it and feel every year of my great age at this moment. Old Johnnie and I've been pals for more years than either of us cares to remember.' He smiled at us, but more at David than myself. 'When you've no less than ten hours to spare I'll tell you how Johnnie Evans-Williams and I won the Second World War together.'

David nodded non-committally. 'Who shot him?'

There was a very faint, very loud, silence. Linda scowled at her muddy legs, Angie flicked back her shoulder-length hair, and Renny shrugged. 'That, dear boy, is the sixty-four-thousand-dollar question. All we can say with any certainty is that it wasn't one of our party.'

'How many's that?' David asked.

'Ten in all. We three, Nick, and the four East Anglian farmers who come together every year, leave their wives behind and keep themselves to themselves. The most we've got out of them is "You all right? That's all right." Decent enough chaps and rattling good shots. Doubt you'll see much of them. They only leave the bar to eat, sleep and shoot and never come in here. Too far from the beer – which reminds me, how about a drink? Trevor'll bring 'em in here but I hope you'll forgive me if I don't join you. I save my one of the day for after dinner. A diabetic for my sins. Rose? I may call you Rose? Delightful name – too close to tea? Oh, how about you, David? No? Linda?'

Linda said she must wait for Nick. Angie pouted and stood up. 'No one's asked me but I want a gin and I'm not drinking alone. I shall brave the heavy mob in the bar.' She gave her lashes another flutter. They were good lashes but her mascara was better as it was intact after a day's shooting. 'You don't mind, do you, Renny, sweetie?'

'My dear,' he said heavily, 'you know I don't.'

'Bless you.' She blew him a kiss and glided off. She moved beautifully.

David glanced after her, then back to Renny. 'Who are the other two?'

'Two?' Renny was lost in thought and had to rouse himself. 'Oh, yes. Old Harry and his boy Mike. Harry's Johnnie's head beater, major-domo and – *entre nous* – our gauleiter. Harbour chap.'

'What exactly happened?' I prompted.

'Well' – he paused to settle himself more comfortably – 'we were all together and had just finished for the day and had our guns down and Johnnie had just joined us and climbed out of our ditch to take a bird from one of the dogs when some lunatic from the dunes behind blasted off and there was old Johnnie's face down in the mud. Very ugly moment.'

'Could've been a bloody sight uglier,' said Linda. 'If

Johnnie hadn't just stooped for that bird he could've lost the back of his head.'

David and I exchanged another glance. I asked, 'Was it a poacher?'

'Your guess is as good as ours, dear lovely little lady. Nick and I rushed for Johnnie, the others charged off to catch the trigger-happy bastard. Not a hope. You could hide a battalion in those dunes and rushes once the light goes.'

David said, 'I take it someone's contacted the cop in Harbour?'

Renny and Linda exchanged glances. She shook her head. 'No. Nick's not happy about that though he can see Johnnie's angle. Johnnie insists he'll not press charges.'

'Understandably,' put in Renny before we could comment. 'This isn't the kind of advertisement Johnnie wants broadcast. And there's another aspect,' he added gravely. 'Once you start pressing charges you can't be sure what you'll turn up. If, as, – *entre nous* – we're all convinced, it was a local chap, old Harry'll find out and sort it out in his own way. But as all these locals are so inbred and interrelated, if he was from Harbour he's bound to be some relative of Harry's. Johnnie needs him too much to upset him by bringing one of his family to court. And – face it – this is the first accident they've had here, though this year, particularly, Johnnie's been afraid one might happen.'

I said, 'Yes, he said that to me this afternoon.'

'That's Johnnie for you. Good chap. Shoots straight, plays straight. However, as he's just said, he's only thankful it was he who copped it and we're thankful it wasn't worse. Johnnie and Helen have sunk their all into this place and worked like beavers to get it going. We've watched them at it from the ground up. Been coming every year since they opened. Before that Angie and I used to stay at the pub in Cornwall they sold to some big brewers to buy this. In point of fact' –

he smiled reminiscently – 'that's where Angie and I met five years ago. She was doing a season in the local rep and used to drop in for a drink. She chucked the stage after we married. The following summer young Linda and Nick were there on honeymoon. Start of a beautiful friendship. They came here on our say-so, now we always come together and, what's more, remain on speaking terms. I must say I look forward to our sojourns on the marsh. Makes a very nice break from the export business. Plastics.' He had a fat man's chuckle. 'What could be more tedious? But that's enough of our life and hard times. May I ask what brings you two charming people here?'

As he had been addressing David, I left it to David.

'Rose is here on doctor's orders and I'm just passing through.'

'From where to where, dear boy?'

'Brisbane to Coventry.'

Even Linda smiled. 'Staying the week?'

'Overnight, far as I know, but I'm not sure that's still on.'

Mrs Evans-Williams chose that moment to come in and announce it was. She was much paler and twisted her beads nervously. 'Nick is such a comfort. He's tucked Johnnie up in bed in the flat, given him a sedative and anti-this and -that jabs and says only flesh wounds and he's got all out, and quite enough in the medical bag he always brings on holiday to stop him going septic, but if he's at all worried in the morning he'll drive Johnnie to Astead General and talk to the casualty officer himself. And Harry has rallied splendidly! He's going to have a camp bed in our office to be on hand for the night. He's just gone back to Harbour to get some night things and tell his wife. Your room is ready for you, Mr Lofthouse, and Johnnie says I'm to tell you if you want it for a few more days you're more than welcome. Just come and sign in whenever it suits you – how about your luggage? – in your car? Oh dear – I've just remembered – all the garages are full – you don't mind leaving it out? It'll be quite safe. Oh, good! You will excuse me – dinner at eight and only one serving as it's Albert's night off and only for residents – do excuse me – ' She scurried away, muttering to herself.

'Fuss, fuss, fuss!' exclaimed Linda. 'Can't think how Johnnie stands it.'

Renny was indulgent. 'Used to it after twenty-odd years. They get along better than most. She's never had kids to use up her energies.' He smiled wryly. 'Not that kids are invariably an unadulterated blessing.'

Linda looked puzzled. 'Thought you got on with your girls, Renny?'

'Now they've married themselves to worthy young men. I'll draw a veil over their teenage years. Twins,' he explained to us, 'and not all that much younger than my dear Angie. I'm afraid their mother and I never hit it off, which didn't precisely enhance the domestic calm. These things happen.' He glanced at me. 'I presume that, like young Linda, you've not yet decided to start a family.'

I shook my head. 'I'm a widow but we didn't have kids.'

David prevented the uncomfortable silence that, as every widow learns, invariably follows that announcement, by saying he hadn't any kids either. 'Far as I know.' He stood up and held out a physical hand. 'Come and help me lug in my stuff, Rose.'

'Sure. If you two'll excuse us?' And, in the corridor, I added, 'You don't have to be so bloody tactful.'

'And you don't have to be so bloody touchy.'

I smiled reluctantly. 'You haven't changed.'

He took my arm and looked towards the hall. 'Nor has

life on the peaceful marsh. Want to get a coat before we brave the outer Arctic?'

'After three years on home territory when there's no blizzard?'

'Like I always said, tough cookies, you Endels. You can carry the heavy one.'

In the hall Mrs Evans-Williams drifted distractedly between counter and propped-open bar door. Trevor was behind the bar drawing pints off the wood for four solid youngish men in rough tweeds with brick-red faces who glanced at us incuriously without interrupting their conversations. Angie had apparently had her gin and vanished.

'Are you sure you can manage those suitcases? I could call Trevor – you can – oh, thank you! I should take you straight up' – Mrs Evans-Williams half-strangled herself with her beads – 'but I'm waiting for a phone call – perhaps a drink first?'

David caught my eye. I didn't know why but read the message. 'If you can give us the key, I can show him up to six, Mrs Evans-Williams.'

'Would you mind? So kind – so kind – many thanks!'

'I've got some rather good duty-free booze in that airline bag you're carrying. Preferable, I thought, to the heavy mob's beery company.' David put down his two large suitcases and cast a cursory glance round the small single room. 'Just the job. And my own bathroom. Someone's told Britain the twentieth century's started.' He went into the bathroom and returned with the tooth glass. 'Just the one. You got another over the way?'

'Two and two armchairs. You haven't got one.'

'Makes a change to be mixing with the well-heeled upper classes.'

I looked pointedly at his discreetly expensive luggage and the matching quality of his well-cut travelling clothes. 'I observe from your threadbare appearance BCC pays its top nuclear physicists peanuts. Come across when you're ready, peasant.'

He tugged his forelock. 'Much obliged, ma'am.'

I laughed and went back to my room.

It was dark outside but as my bedroom curtains were open the reflections from the electrified coachlamps in the yard provided enough light for me to draw my curtains before turning on mine. I was about to deal first with the two windows overlooking the yard, when I saw a man coming out of the small side door at the far end of the five garage doors. He was shortish and thickset, carrying a small dark briefcase, and walked towards the main entrance with the stooping shoulders and downcast head of a doctor thinking over the case he had just left. The rays of the coachlight by the reception entrance were on him when he shook his head at his thoughts, and from the expression on his pleasantly plain face he was more puzzled than anxious. Not wishing to advertise the fact that I was watching, I waited until he was inside before drawing the curtains, then paused again. Another figure had glided from the shadows at the other end of the garage. I recognized the graceful walk before I saw Angie le Vere's face in the coachlights. She looked extraordinarily happy. Well, well, I thought, standing back a little, until she disappeared not into reception but by a side door further on which, as I recalled, was just beyond the telephone alcove. Purely from amused curiosity, I went to my marsh window for a look at the road and just glimpsed the outline of a man walking swiftly towards the sea.

'Recognize him?' queried David when he poured the drinks.

'Too far off. Nor, to be honest, does there have to be any connection, but – '

'It's just our nasty, suspicious minds, love – and our

Angie's lean and hungry look. Cheers, Rosie. Nice to see you again.'

'And you. Tell me about Australia.'

We forgot the time and were late for dinner. Mrs Evans-Williams had no doubts what had kept us. She flushed and announced coyly that we hadn't seen each other for a long time. In the dining room the ubiquitous Trevor in a waiter's suit smirked knowingly as he showed us to our table. David glanced at him, then bent tenderly towards me. 'No regrets, Rose?' Trevor skipped away for the menu with the back of his neck bright red. I kicked David under the table and exchanged smiles with the le Veres who were sitting with the McCabes. The latter had their backs to us and when they both turned to nod politely I recognized the face of the man I had seen in the yard. The four farmers at the only other occupied table ignored us and everyone else and only opened their mouths to shovel in more food and beer. I was suddenly very glad David was with me. Normally I never minded being alone or eating alone, but, possibly consequent on Johnnie's injury, there was an atmosphere in that dining room that I didn't like. The silences at the other tables were too tense and the brief periods of conversation between the le Veres and McCabes too artificial. But the food was very good and, if the service was slow as Trevor was on his own, at least he seemed oblivious to the atmosphere.

'Would be Albert's night off, wouldn't it? Albert, he's head waiter like and normal when he's off the guv'nor lends a hand dinners. Other nights the guv'nor watches the bar. I mean, not a job for the missus on her own. You never know this far out, do you? The missus, she's got to watch the hall — not that we gets much visiting trade the duck season. Got our hands full, the guv'nor says, without letting in a shower of non-residents, but we always keep the three tables for when the guv'nor obliges special for dinners. Most nights we've the two or three taken but not tonight. The missus, she's not got no bookings for tonight and she's not taking none neither seeing as we not even got young Mike helping out the kitchen. Cruel shook up he was seemly after seeing the guv'nor get it. Old Harry he fetched him back home but he's back now watching the bar. He'll not set foot in here nor the kitchens. Reckons meals is women's work, Harry does.'

'You don't, Trevor?'

His pale, sharp face was intelligent and crafty. 'Not me, madam. I'm here to learn the hotel trade proper. Have me own one day I will. Come down from London last year, see, and I not been here the year without catching on as it's the bar as makes the lolly and the dining room as makes the reputation. Steak to your liking, madam? And you, sir? That's nice. What'll it be to follow? Apple pie with cream, blackberry flan, crème caramel or the cheese board straight?'

After we'd ordered, David asked, 'Trevor not Trev, lad?'

Trevor winked. 'Trevor, sir. The missus she reckons Trev not got the class and I reckons she's right. If you wants the carriage trade, she says, you got to have class.' He eyed the farmers disdainfully. 'Mind you, these days, you got the lolly you got the class. Not but what the guv'nor says you'll not find many a better shot than them four – er – gentlemen.' He lowered his voice conspiratorially. 'You'll not find a better nowhere than that Mr le Vere, the guv'nor reckons. He was with him one time Bisley when that Mr le Vere hit the bull's eye the fifty times out the fifty with a .303 and as good with a shotgun he is as with a rifle. Taught his missus hisself he did and the guv'nor reckons she's the best lady shot he's come across. That Mrs McCabe, well, she's still learning like but coming along real nice seemly and the doctor he's hot stuff. Seems as his dad taught him going after moose when he was a nipper – moose, I ask you. Then duck. Did you ever? Cheese board, Mr le Vere? Just coming, sir!'

David watched him skip away. 'He's dead keen **we** shouldn't pin Johnnie's peppering on one of this lot.'

'You think?'

His sleepy eyes met mine. 'Just an impression. I'm suddenly too bloody tired to think.' He stifled a yawn. 'Delayed-action jet-lag plus that good wine.'

'And that good pre-dinner whisky. Why not skip coffee and go straight to bed?'

'You wouldn't mind?'

'Of course not. I won't hang on down here much longer. I can't take much more shooting talk. I'm not sure about this coming week.'

'Let's leave the agonizing reappraisal till morning.'

'Sure.' I looked at him more closely. 'Poor man, you do look whacked.'

'I am.' He smiled apologetically. 'Just as well I'm sleeping alone. Dead loss to one and all elsewhere.'

Renny came over as David rose. 'Leaving us, dear boy? Jet-lag? You've all my sympathy. I'll see you out as I'm off to the bar for our liquers. It'll save young Trevor a little running. You'll join us, Rose? Coffee and liqueurs in the lounge – but I insist! What'll it be? Drambuie? Coming up!'

Angie swept over and swept me into the lounge. She had changed into a black evening sweater and tight black velvet pants. She looked good, if not quite as young as I had first thought her. She acted young and she acted well. When she had poured herself into an armchair I asked about her stage career.

Her big eyes widened. 'Sweetie, you can't have heard of me! How did you know?'

'Your husband told us earlier.'

She smiled widely. 'Bless him! It's no use kidding – I was the world's lousiest actress as I kept forgetting my words.

Natch, there was a time when I thought I was the white hope of the British theatre – who doesn't think that at drama school? And I usually got work as I was quite good at character-bits as I can mimic. My first taught me. He was an impressionist.'

'Your first husband?'

'Natch, sweetie. He was fabulous guy – hell to live with – did I make a boo-boo when I married him – but who doesn't? And you're a widow? How many times?'

I was only momentarily taken aback, and more by the novelty of her query than anything else. It was very much the kind of thing Sue Denver would have said. 'Once.'

She spread her arms gracefully. 'Don't let it bug you. Years ahead and half the human race to pick from.' The McCabes had come in. 'You haven't met Nick.' She smiled up at him through her lashes. 'Our fabulous Nick from Toronto.'

'Ottawa,' Nick McCabe corrected pleasantly. Linda ignored us, dropped on to the corner of a sofa and pointedly opened an erudite paperback.

Nick sat by me, and in his slow, pedantic, but not unattractive Canadian drawl told me a little of his job in a northern teaching hospital and then a great deal about Canada. It was my night for colonial travelogues, but by the time we reached Vancouver I couldn't have borne another mile on the Canadian Pacific railroad. Earlier, David had left me with an urgent desire to see Queensland, what he called 'the Gulf country' and New South Wales.

Renny le Vere had barely spoken since he came in with our liqueurs and nor, I noticed had he or Angie looked at each other. That didn't surprise me as I had seen so many of my married friends suffering from the same syndrome once the first enthusiasm had worn off and they had discovered they had little in common and nothing left to say to each other. The McCabes didn't talk much together but their mutual attitude was totally different. They didn't have to talk as their frequent mutual glances were carrying on the private unspoken conversation of two people still in love with each other. Nick's behaviour reminded me of Francis Denver. Francis was seldom able to keep his eyes off his wife.

Renny came out of his reverie to ask, 'Where precisely do you live, Rose?'

I took him over to the map. 'There.'

His expression quickened. 'On Midstreet Marsh?'

'You know Midstreet?'

'Not at first hand.' He studied the map more keenly. 'Someone – some chap in the bar a few nights back – mentioned living there and told us about the village being washed away. What was his name?' he mused. 'Used to drop in occasionally last year – slight, quiet chap with reddish hair and clever eyes – Dexter?'

'Denver? Francis Denver?'

He smiled at me. 'Yes. I think that's the name.' He glanced round. 'Angie, my dear – Francis Denver? Ring a bell?'

Angie turned slowly. 'Should it, sweetie? Oh, yes!' She slapped her forehead. 'I know who you mean! That guy in the bar last week – something to do with mines – you used to chat with him last year. Runs a Jag.'

I said, 'A red Audi now.'

'Sweetie, I wouldn't know. Only cars I recognize are Jags as Renny had one when we first met.'

'Jags and Rolls,' put in Renny dryly.

She flung back her head and laughed. 'Natch! What woman doesn't notice a Rolls?' She returned to the long conversation she had started with Nick. I couldn't tell if he was enjoying it. Linda wasn't.

Renny asked, 'Denver a friend of yours, Rose?'

'Oh, yes. Francis and Sue Denver are my nearest neighbours. They drove over with me this afternoon.'

He nodded pleasantly, returned his attention to the map and asked more about the marsh. We went back to our seats discussing crops and tides.

Angie broke in, 'Must be fabulous living on the marsh all the year, but if you don't shoot – why come here?'

'Line of least resistance.' I explained myself and used my flu as an excuse to get away. 'Still a bit cotton-woolly. Do you all mind?'

Renny rose. 'I think we should follow your good example as we've to rise at the unmentionable hour of four-thirty. Coming, dear people?'

Trevor arrived for our cups and glasses as we were leaving. Renny laid a hand on his arm. 'Delicious coffee. Thank you.'

'Glad it suited, sir.' Trevor flicked his arm free and went on with his collecting. Out of the corner of my eye I saw the McCabes stare at the floor and Angie's face harden. I was suddenly much more in sympathy with her desire for fresh air before dinner.

The farmers were still in the bar and Mrs Evans-Williams still in the hall. She was talking to a small, leathery middle-aged man wearing an old tweed cap jammed over his eyes and muddy wellingtons with the tops turned down – the insignia of a marsh-dweller. She told us Johnnie was resting comfortably and introduced me to her companion. 'You must meet Harry!' She used the tone others reserve for the Almighty. 'Harry is our right hand and how we need him now! Harry, this is the young lady from Endel I've been telling you about.'

Harry gave me an unsmiling glance and lifted his cap just long enough to expose his almost obscenely white bald head and fringe of grey-black at the back. ' 'Evening, madam.' He slapped back the cap.

'Good evening,' I said.

My companions exchanged amused glances and, on the first floor passage, congratulated me. 'We've never seen Harry shift his cap to any woman before,' said Linda.

Angie sighed dramatically. 'Hell, you and I aren't loaded young widows, sweetie.'

I felt very post-fluish. 'It's not that. It's just that Harry and I are both indigenous natives. What's his surname? Mercer, Gillion, Wenden, Wattle, Smith, Burt, Endel?'

'Wattle!' Nick McCabe was enchanted. 'Can you imagine! Harry Wattle. Are you saying there are more Wattles elsewhere on this Marsh?'

'Hordes. A third of my nearest village are Wattles.'

Renny said it was all quite fascinating and we must have another long chat tomorrow evening. 'Alas, dear girl, we are all ignorant aliens, but not enemy aliens, I trust.' He held back my fire doors for me. 'Good night and sweet sleep.'

It was undoubtedly the flu, but as the doors swung shut I shivered and was irrationally relieved to see from the chink under the door that David's light was still on. From the silence he was either in the bath or had fallen asleep reading in bed as he must have heard me unlock my door but didn't call another good night.

Someone had been into my room to wash glasses and empty the ashtray while we were at dinner. Whoever it was was honest. The level of the whisky in the bottle on my dressing-table was much as I remembered and only the twenty David had removed had gone from the carton of duty-free king-sizes. I was about to put both on my side table when I remembered the number that David smoked daily, that he used to be an early riser and as that twenty was bound to be down to single figures by now, unless I wanted to be woken at dawn by David panting to shorten his life, I had better take them over while his light was on.

I closed but didn't bother to lock my door and knocked on his. No answer. I knocked more loudly as he was obviously in the bathroom. No answer. I cursed him as I wanted to go to bed, and without much hope tried the door. To my surprise it was unlocked. I intended opening it just wide enough to push in his property when I saw him sprawled asleep on top of his bed fully dressed apart from his shoes. From the clouds of steam issuing from the open darkened bathroom, he had filled the bath before dropping off so quickly he hadn't even removed his glasses and they'd fallen forward on to his chin.

I went in quietly, took off his glasses and was putting them by his room key on the bedside table when he woke, raised himself on an elbow and blinked blearily. 'Is this where I start believing in miracles, Rose?'

'No.' I told him why I was there. 'Sorry,' I went on, 'to have woken you, but you'll be more comfortable in, than on, the bed.'

'Yes. Thanks.' He reached, groaning, for his glasses. 'Christ, I feel awful. I was about to have a bath but put in so much hot I couldn't get my hand down to the plug and the chain's busted.' He glanced at the bathroom. 'You turn off that light?'

'No. Off when I came in. You must've and forgotten.'

'I don't think I did. No. Sure I didn't. I wanted it on for the piglights to heat it up.'

'Piglights?'

He got off the bed. 'Those large round lights hanging from the ceiling double as heaters. You've got two over the way. They use them in pigsties in winter. Useful jobs. I'll show you.' He walked over in his socks, put up a hand towards the switch outside the bathroom door, then drew his hand back sharply and without moving forward peered i..to the darkened room. He didn't say anything until he had found and flicked on his lighter and held it forward. 'Correction, Rose,' he said flatly, 'this is where I start believing in miracles. Come here' – he grabbed my arm – 'only for Christ's sake don't touch that switch or go into the bathroom until we're sure the main fuse has blown and that all the wiring in there is as dead as I'd now be had I not chosen to spend a few minutes thinking on this and that while my bath water cooled off.'

For a moment I didn't believe him. And then I had to believe him. In the lighter's flickering flame I saw the wires trailing from the sagging patch of ceiling plaster to the two broad shallow objects bobbing in the bath water. 'Oh, my God. You're right. You could've been killed.'

'Yep.' He looked as shaken as I felt. 'Me and Johnnie in one evening. I wonder who'll collect the third near-miss before tonight's out?'

I was too upset for conscious thought so what I said came out of my subconscious. It astonished me as much as David. 'Think there'll be a third? Or that this one was meant for Johnnie too?'

3

The pre-dawn sky was black and starless when I was woken with a start by the footsteps in the yard. Angie le Vere's stage whisper floated up to my open window. 'My God, sweeties, if this isn't grounds for divorce I don't know what is.'

I hauled the bedclothes over my head until the sound of cars crawling off faded in the distance. I felt very sorry for the ducks. The poor little things hadn't a chance with all those determined marksmen and sharp-shooting wives setting out to finish them off.

What were Johnnie Evans-Williams's chances of surviving a third? Or was David right and all that ailed me a combination of post-flu depression and the ghosts his return had raised for me? 'Maybe I should've stayed out of your life,' he said. 'Maybe the kindest thing I can do for us both is to move out tomorrow and stay out. Obviously, that'll be the most sensible thing to do if the sight of me has you seeing murderers lurking behind every door, even although, as you've just said, until tonight it's not occurred to you to so much as smell skullduggery since Endel caved in. But if it'll ease your mind for the moment, let's play this your way. Give me a hand shoving that little dressing chest across this open door to stop me stumbling in half-asleep. If it was set up, whoever did it set it to look like an accident and won't be back tonight. He or she'll have to sweat it out until the result in your imagination is announced by the screams of Mrs Wassname-Wassname or the room maid using the pass key to find out why the gaffer hasn't showed up and finds him starkers in the bath with his head touching his heels. Right?' I said nothing. From the look he gave me he thought I needed a very good psychiatrist. 'After I've had some sleep,' he continued, 'I'll report this in daylight, insist on taking first look at the main fuse box and then I'll make a thorough check' – he jerked a thumb – 'in there. All right?'

'Yes,' I lied. 'I expect you're right. You always used to be right. Just flu. You don't have to push off tomorrow.'

'Let's talk about that one tomorrow, love.'

The outburst of notes from the first rising lark was a glorious relief. The birds subscribed to the established order and, once the larks had declared the new day, at first sleepily, then in full voice, the others joined in. The chorus was interwoven by the croaking of the frogs, the goat-like grunts of the snipe on the wing and the cynical ha-ha-has of the wheeling gulls. And the plaintive peewits and pee-ip, pee-ip, pee-ips of the lapwing and plover sang a requiem for the ducks.

With a little less luck this morning two dead men could have earned that requiem. By sheer luck Johnnie had stooped for that bird; by sheer luck David had been so tired he had forgotten to lock his door and flaked out.

Daylight came wrapped in a gentle mist. Then more glorious sounds. Motor-bike and moped engines and human voices saying good morning and wasn't it shocking about poor Mr Evans-Williams and didn't it just go to show there wasn't no telling there wasn't.

I got up and had a long bath and when I got back found a morning tea-tray by my bed. No newspapers yet. The papers came out with the bread in the milkman's van at mid-morning. I saw the mail van coming down the road from Harbour as I drank my tea and felt much more normal. My post at home came out twice a day in the mail van from St Martin's that called first at the Denvers', then Walt

45

Ames's house on the farm, last at Endel, then turned back to the village. We all used the postman-drivers as our private pony express as they never minded delivering verbal messages with the mail, invariably did so correctly, and so often our telephones were dead, as gales, or the wide wings of swans, had brought down the wires.

My mind drifted off to a black and white drawing of a swan I'd bought at last year's Cliffhill Art Soc. exhibition – oh, my God! It was this afternoon. If I didn't show up Mrs Smith would never forgive me. She was a good, God-fearing, well-meaning, stupid, insensitive woman and didn't like me, though for social reasons she made a civilized pretence of so doing. Unless I were on my death-bed, her umbrage over my absence would be beyond bearing, and tough on Mr Smith, whom I liked. I felt he liked me, even if he didn't always like my decisions. His one consolation over my will had been his conviction that women invariably changed their minds.

There was no sound from David's room when I stopped outside his door on my way to breakfast and the postcard he had inscribed in capitals PLEASE DO NOT DISTURB hung from the handle. I looked at it momentarily, then knocked. 'No tea, thanks,' he grunted. I breathed out, told myself to stop being so damned neurotic and went on down. The front hall was empty. I had a solitary meal in the dining room served by a chubby, fresh-faced young woman in a pink nylon button-through over hand-knit and jeans. She said her name was Hilda, and that she was from Harbour, came out weekday mornings with Doreen who did upstairs, and nothing else. She knew only ignorant foreigners talked at breakfast. Her silence was amiable, the food even better than at dinner, and the atmosphere even better still. I would have enjoyed my meal much more had that second improvement not been so noticeable.

David's notice was still up when I got back and Doreen was cleaning my room. She was considerably older than Hilda, and wore the same pink over a different-coloured hand-knit and the same jeans. Breakfast was over so conversation in order. 'From Midstreet aren't you, madam? You have come to a home from home, haven't you? Wasn't it shocking about poor Mr Evans-Williams? Could've been killed, Harry says, and the cruel turn it give that poor young Mike. Sensitive he is. Teenager. Well, I mean some of 'em are and some of 'em aren't and I should know having the three and the noise – you'd not credit it, madam – but like hubby says you're only young the once – and it's a wonder to him, he says, as there's not been more accidents down Harbour Marsh what with all these poachers coming down from Astead and Cliffhill and London, hubby shouldn't wonder, and not paying no shooting dues neither nor knowing one end of a gun from the other proper.'

'So you've had a lot of poachers down here?'

'That's what the men says up the Anchor at Harbour – but you know men, madam, say anything they will when they've had a few – but where's the harm a working man enjoying his pint? Sleep well, did you, madam? That's good. Been poorly, Mrs Evans-Williams says, needing a nice rest and you'll get that here. Ever so quiet once the guns gone.' She nodded her curly grey head at the door. 'I left your gentleman friend be. You leave him till he wakes, Mrs Evans-Williams says, been travelling he has and needs his sleep. All right if I do your bathroom now?'

'Sure.' I followed her in to admire the décor. 'Very attractive wall tiles. Same in all these bathrooms?'

'In different colours, madam.' She scattered scouring powder as the sower his seeds. 'Mr Evans-Williams had a firm down from London do the lot. He's asked first for Biggs of Cliffhill but they couldn't fit the time with him. Nice enough chaps he fetched down and hard workers, but I'm glad as wasn't me as had to foot the bill. Nothing but the best for Mr Evans-Williams. Ever so particular, he is.'

'Shows. I suppose they did six as well?'

'Finished up in there. Well, he says, don't want to spoil the ship for a ha'porth of tar and could come in useful having the extra private bath if we've to let it special.'

'So it's often let?'

'I'd not say often. Just when Mrs Evans-Williams obliges special like for your gentleman friend or one of the business gentlemen as come down to see him.'

'Reps?'

Doreen was shocked. 'Oh, no, madam! Not Harbour Inn. No commercials, no coaches. Rule of the house.' She turned on the bath taps.

I left her to it, went back into the corridor, closed my door and knocked loudly on David's. 'David. Rose. You awake?'

'No,' he groaned, 'dead. Hold on – ' I heard him cursing for his glasses then stumbling for the door. 'Christ, woman, can't you read?'

'Yes, but I've had breakfast. Can I come in a moment?' I pushed him back without waiting for an answer, went in, closed and leant against his door. 'I – I thought I'd take a walk,' I invented, 'then wondered if you'd rather I stayed around when you report' – I glanced towards his bathroom – 'that lot.'

He ruffled his untidy head and considered me quizzically. 'Thanks, love, but I'm a big boy now. I can wash behind my own ears and mend a fuse. You take a walk and draw some pretty bird pictures.'

I looked him in the face. 'And give you a chance to ring the nearest psychiatrist? Okay. I'll take my walk.' I only then noticed his pyjamas. 'My God. Where did you get those?'

His pyjamas were black silk, piped and monogrammed on all three pockets in gold.

He said reproachfully, 'I'd have you know these are Hong Kong's best custom-built jobs.'

I shook my head sadly. 'You were quite right not to marry her, David.'

He held open the door, grinning. 'Get out and leave me to me beautiful memories.'

I pushed a small sketching pad and handful of pencils into my anorak pocket. I wasn't in my da Vinci mood, but sketching usually helped me to think more clearly and my mind was badly in need of clarification. The hall was still empty when I deposited my key on the counter, and somewhere behind the swing door Mrs Evans-Williams was discussing a laundry problem with Hilda. '. . . If the van doesn't arrive on time you must re-lay with red damask all round as we must have matching cloths and napkins. Do try and remember, please, Hilda, napkins not serviettes. These little details make all the difference and you know how particular Mr Evans-Williams is about little details . . . .'

Very particular man, Mr Evans-Williams, but not one to fuss over the identity of the person who just missed blowing his head off. I wondered how particular he would be over a little detail such as death by electrocution?

He came out of the side door by the garages when I walked into the otherwise empty yard. His right arm was in a sling and from his appearance and walk he had aged ten years overnight. After we'd exchanged civilities and I had had his version of what had happened – which tallied almost word for word with Renny le Vere's account – he added, 'Talk about being hoist with my own petard after warning you, eh?'

'I thought that last night. Very tough on you. Should you be up today? Forgive me, but you look as if the shock's not yet worn off.'

His bloodshot eyes were grateful. 'Many thanks for the kind thought, Mrs D. Between ourselves and that sign up there, nothing I'd like more than today with my feet up. But young Nick McCabe said it wouldn't hurt me to potter around and could do what remains of my lungs some good as I refuse to stop smoking. I can't slack off today. Not fair to leave Helen to run the shop alone when we're full. Three hands are better than two, especially today. Brewer's delivery's due. Cellar's my pigeon. We've got to get all the empty barrels up and leave new space below. The lorry's due out this morning but most likely won't appear till afternoon unless we're not ready for it! No peace for the wicked eh?' He nodded at David's white car. 'Mr Lofthouse still got his head down?'

I watched his face closely in the gentle sunlight. 'I've just woken him.'

'Thank you for it?'

'Not effusively.'

He grinned boyishly and again, as yesterday, I was conscious that something about him struck a chord. I still couldn't place it. 'Travelling by air exhausts the strongest. Has he decided to stay on?'

'I'm not sure. He was far too tired last night to think of anything but sleep.'

Had I not been watching him so closely I would have missed the relief that flickered at the back of his eyes. 'Far as we're concerned, he's most welcome as I'm walking wounded. Where are you off to now?'

'Just taking a stroll till he's up and about. Where shouldn't I go?'

He cocked his head, then twisted it around so like an Alsatian scenting danger that I expected his ears and hackles to shoot up. 'Harry took the dawn patrol to meet the flights coming in north-east – just a few miles south of Lymchurch.

Thataway. If you keep sou'-east you should have the old harbour to yourself. Should be pleasant walking now the sun's breaking through.'

I paused on the bridge beyond the cinder road to look back at the inn buildings lying peacefully in the morning sun. The weatherboarding was freshly whitewashed, the black cross-beams and doors were freshly oiled; the ancient, dark-brown roof-tiles of the inn and new ugly grey slates on the outhouses were in good repair and the grey-white stone flags of the yard were swept clean. It only needed roses round the doors and the oldest inhabitant in his smock with his pint on the black wrought-iron bench drawn up against the bar wall to be a natural for a Come To Beautiful Britain poster.

I recognized the workmanship of that bench. It had been made by the blacksmith in Coxden, the mainland village nearest the marsh that lay roughly midway between Astead and Cliffhill. I thought the Evans-Williamses had been wise to patronize local craftsmen where they could. Any incomers who spent money locally and provided regular jobs for local labour were far more likely to overcome the initial resentment towards newcomers that was an instinctive reaction in close-knit rural communities, and gain, if never acceptance, at least a not inconsiderable degree of respect. And then as I strolled on I found myself recalling that, while marshfolk were seldom averse to making a fast buck out of strangers and had their vices, these did not usually include biting the hands that fed them.

Of course, that poacher could've come from Astead, Cliffhill, London . . . and if he had come from the mainland Harry Wattle would have had him in the nick last night. Possibly one could hide a battalion in those dunes once the light went, but not a solitary or small posse of strangers from a crafty, experienced old marshman on his home marsh.

Walt Ames was about Harry's age; at any hour of the day or night, unless there was a real mist, Walt could pinpoint to within a few yards the whereabouts of every stranger on Midstreet Marsh. I once asked him how he did it. 'Either I smells 'em,' he said, 'or me dogs do.'

Dogs. Harry had had his dogs last night. Why hadn't he used them? Obvious. No stranger. Still more obvious, Harry hadn't wanted him found – which was precisely what Renny had said. Maybe I should find that psychiatrist for myself.

The sun had dispersed the mist and left behind a queer greenish undersea light that hung over the flat fields and topaz dykes. The self-planted hawthorn and wind-stunted willows that trailed into the water and the orange heads of the reed-mace looked stiff as coral and as if they sheltered fishes not birds. But in every dyke the moorhens scuttled over the water, rootled in the rushes, and in every field the lapwing and plover were black and white smudges. High above, the wide empty sky reflected the pale-blue serenity of the murmuring sea. I counted five herons, each fishing one-legged in its own private dyke, and lost count of the pheasants ambling on to the road, and the magpies. To see just one magpie was bad luck; a pair, good luck. I saw so many pairs stomping over the grass like elderly clerics soberly conversing at some massive ecclesiastical convention that my marsh blood was convinced God was in his heaven and all was right with my world. Unfortunately, I was only half-marsh. I stopped on another bridge for another anxious look back at the inn and immediately had that uncomfortable sensation of being watched by someone unseen. Then I remembered that was only too likely as I was in sight of the inn and Doreen or anyone else might quite reasonably be watching me from an upper window.

I lost interest in the subject in my new interest in the outline of the old harbour that from where I stood was as clear as a line drawn on a map. The inn and two old nethouses marked the left arm, a trio of even more derelict nethouses, the right. Those nethouses had been built by the fishermen who used them to dry, make and store their nets, were shaped much like stone beehives about six or seven feet wide at the base and not much more than five feet high. The men who had built them had been the men who had walked with ease in and out of the old doors of the inn. There were similar old nethouses dotted all round the coast and most were used by shepherds to house fodder for straying, hungry sheep.

A footpath ran down from the left of that bridge to skirt the inland edge of a cross-dyke, meander round a nethouse and then stop abruptly in the middle of the field beyond. The field on the far side of the cross-dyke stretched to the sea road and was less green and much more broken with patches of sand, pebbles, sea-pinks and saltwater pools. I took the footpath and my time. The sun was warmer; the greenish light had gone; the air was crisp with salt, and alive with the soft cries and chatter of birds and the soft whisper of the sea. The beauty and the tranquillity seeped into me and dispersed all confused thoughts of dangers past and present, as the sun the morning mist.

I pushed open the rotting wooden door of the nethouse and peered inside. The pile of stale fodder seemed to have been flattened into a mattress by human hands and was oddly patched with a greenish-purple fuzz. I propped open the door to let in more light and touched one patch gingerly, thinking it must be a fungus I didn't recognize. I was glad there was no one around to see my error and grinned at myself. The 'fungus' was mohair and had obviously rubbed off some girl's coat. Young love from Harbour needing privacy and shelter when it was too cold for haystacks and Dutch barns and the blood was too hot to be bothered by the musty smell, and the fleas and spiders in that fodder. I wasn't in love and I was terrified of spiders. I ducked back outside, and absently thrust my handful of mohair into one of my anorak pockets as the moorhens scurried for cover. I sat down on a sandy patch outside, leant back against the hut and after a very few minutes the moorhens forgot I was there.

I had spent over an hour making desultory sketches when a cormorant suddenly poised on the bridge wall with bronze-black wings displayed. His brownish-white instead of pristine white headdress showed that winter was near and his mating season temporarily over. He had vanished, and I was shading the head and wondering if I would wear brownish white permanently, when David loomed over me hugging himself in his overcoat. 'Why aren't your hands too frost-bitten to draw, Rose?'

'My, my, that Australian sun has thinned your blood.' I closed my sketching pad. 'Meanwhile, back at the ranch . . .?'

He smiled apologetically, ducked to look inside the net-house, ducked out and sat by me. 'I've just left old Johnnie blowing all fuses and his lovely wife having hysterics. He's threatening to sue the electrical firm, the South-Eastern Electricity Board, the Government, the architects, the decorators, the plumber, the plumber's mate and the lad who makes the tea – just for starters. Can't say I blame him. The coroner's remarks wouldn't have done his trade too much good. As he said, he's the bloke that foots the bill.'

'Genuine faulty fixture?'

'From all the evidence I've seen and I've had a good look. I'd say they cut corners in that bathroom as in the bedroom, finished off in a hurry and weren't too fussy check-ing the beams were strong enough to hold the fixture. Old beams. Look strong enough until you start shoving in a

54

knife. After a slightly sticky start my penknife went in like butter.' He looked at me. 'You know how these very old beams can look tough as hell on the outside and be crumbling inside.'

'Just that?'

'That's how it looks and what I'll have to say on oath if it comes to court. Johnnie asked if I'll speak up for him. I've said I will. Not that I think it'll come to that unless I sue for my damaged nervous system, which I won't. Thanks to you, I'm still the lad I've always known and loved. I can't see either party wanting the bad publicity. They'll settle out. Incidentally, I'm giving you the news now. Johnnie was so worked-up at the prospect of your reaction that I didn't want to make certain of his stroke by telling him the truth.'

I coloured. 'Thanks. I don't much mind your seeing me with egg on my face but I'd rather that wasn't general knowledge.'

'We all have our off moments, love.' He lit a cigarette and spent a couple of minutes watching the moorhens. 'If those holding screws had been loosened intentionally I would have expected them to come out much more cleanly.'

I turned to him sharply. 'It did cross your mind to wonder if I was right?'

'You know my nasty, suspicious mind. Of course it did, especially as I could've been at the receiving end. Though I thought, and think, yours was a daft theory, I allowed for the possibility that it might be right to save myself from later having to beat my breast for helping to dig old Johnnie's grave. I honestly now think you can scrub that one out, and quite as much from his immediate reaction as anything else. I don't know him, but I do know an angry bloke when I see one. He was bloody angry but not scared angry. Just good honest this-hits-me-in-the-pocket angry.'

'A nice healthy reaction.'

'So why hasn't it made you feel nice and healthy?' He blinked over his glasses and I could almost see the computer flicking over. 'It's not Johnnie, is it?' He tapped his chest. 'Johnnie's offered to knock twenty per cent off the bill if I stay. I told him I wasn't sure yet. I am now. I think,' he said gently, 'I'll push off for Coventry after lunch.'

I didn't say anything at once. My judgement agreed with him. My instincts didn't. I decided on a compromise. 'Must you go today? Couldn't you leave it till tomorrow?'

'Give me one good reason for that suggestion?'

I smiled suddenly. 'I've got one. I want you to come and hold my hand at Cliffhill Art Soc.'s annual exhibition this afternoon.'

'You want – WHAT?'

I explained in detail. 'Be a chum, David,' I went on, 'and come. It's going to be hell but I must go and with you there I can get away earlier. And then why don't we have dinner somewhere well away from dead birds? If we're about to part for ever again, for God's sake let's celebrate.'

He began to laugh. 'A greater love for woman hath no man,' he spluttered, 'than the man who lets himself be dragged kicking and screaming to culture. Right. We'll sing our swan-song *chez* Cliffhill Art Soc., then I'll wine and dine you, kiss you sadly on both cheeks and vanish into the night – at a civilized hour before lunch tomorrow. Hat and white gloves?'

'Darling, please' – I mimicked Sue Denver's affected drawl – 'do remember you're back in England. Handblocked silk headscarf, handmade brogues, pigskin sling-bag and gloves and Harris tweeds, of course.'

He touched my boots. 'You mean I'm actually going to see your legs the once before the great farewell? Oh me blood-pressure! Down hormones, down!' He stood up, slapping himself. 'If I don't move, I won't live for the erotic thrill. You'll have to strew me frozen corpse with rushes and sing a sad song. If we're going to have a knees-up, I suppose you'll want me to drive?'

'Yes, please. My car or yours?'

'Mine as she's still running in. The sooner I get her over that stage the better. How far is it? I've forgotten.'

'Thirty-three miles.'

'She'll need petrol.' He glanced at his watch. 'Half-eleven. I presume there's a garage in Harbour. I'll walk back now and run her up as we've to leave early after lunch.' He glanced round at the sound of the first car coming down the road since I had left the inn. 'Looks like someone looking for someone – oh, aye – I know that face. One red Audi slowing at the bridge.' He raised his voice. ' 'Morning, Francis! If you're looking for Rose, she's sitting at my feet.'

I heard Francis Denver's amazed shout, 'I say, old chap, what a memory! Hallo there, David! Welcome to the marsh! They said at the inn that Rose was around. I suppose you don't know if my wife's rung her?'

'Oh, no,' I muttered, 'now what am I not meant to say?' I stood up, scattering sketch pad and pencils. David dived for them as Francis joined us. 'Hi, Francis. Did Sue say she'd ring me?'

'She said something about it at breakfast just before she took off for Astead on two wheels to keep a hairdressing date.' Francis draped himself against the nethouse. He was a couple of years older than David but looked younger as his long thin sensitive face had the thick-skinned unlined pallor that occasionally accompanies dark-red hair and dark-blue eyes. He was the only man I knew who could look elegant in tweeds even when his feet were in turned-down wellingtons. 'We agreed I'd drop in on you on my way to Cliffhill. I'm due there at twelve. I'll be late,' he smiled pleasantly, 'but worth it. We weren't too happy to leave you just like that yesterday and, from what I've just seen of the inn, I'm even less happy. State of chaos up there. Damned glad you're here to keep an eye on Rose, David. We heard from Walt Ames last night that you were back and had come over. How are you?'

'Great, thanks. And so, from the sound of it, is the marsh bush-telegraph.'

'It does its job. But how does this chap do it, Rose? Must be three years since we last had a drink and he gets my name at sight. I can hardly remember the names of the people with whom I'd drinks last week.'

'That reminds me!' I told him about the le Veres. 'Renny's large, middle-aged, big-business – Angie, his wife, lots younger, dark, very slim, very attractive, wouldn't you say, David?'

'What I'd say,' said David, 'is dead sexy if you fancy angles and not curves and some do.'

Francis frowned slightly, then grinned. 'I know who you mean. Yes. I'm with you, David. But, about Sue, if she gets in touch or if not this afternoon, could you tell her that, instead of just having a late lunch with her father and then going back home as I said I would, I'm going to court with him. He rang me just after she'd left to say he'd got Mercer v. Mercer coming off this afternoon as I'd asked him to let me know. Should be worth hearing, don't you agree, Rose?'

'Wow! Yes.' I turned to David. 'Tom and Ron Mercer are brothers who haven't spoken to each other for years. Family relations weren't improved when Tom shot Ron's prize Alsatian bitch because she somehow – and no one seems to know how – got among his sheep. She didn't attack any but Tom vows they were all ewes in lamb and he couldn't take chances. You can guess what Ron says. He's sueing his brother. Split St Martin's down the middle. But, Francis, I thought the case was coming off next week?'

'It seems to have been brought forward to this afternoon. I've no idea why. My father-in-law is a man of great discretion and – er – wisdom. As he remarked this morning, most regrettably he has to miss Cliffhill exhibition.'

I laughed. 'I adore Mr Smith. I'm taking David.'

'My God, you're not! David, you're a brave man.'

'And I know it. What's worse, I'm dying of cold.'

I said, 'He thinks this the frozen north after the outback.'

'Outback? Of course. I'd forgotten you'd been there. Where were you based? Brisbane, didn't Rose say?'

'Occasionally,' said David, watching us both.

'What was it like?'

'Lovely bloody hot.' David moved away up the path.

'Want a lift back? I'll run you both up.' Francis and I followed slowly. He smiled at David's back. 'Sue's already working on her wedding outfit.'

'Don't let her lay out any lolly on it unless you want to waste it.'

'You sound as if you mean that, Rose.'

'You should know me well enough by now to know that I do.'

He was a nice, kind-hearted, intelligent man. But a man. 'If you say so, my dear,' he said in the tone men use at such moments.

'I do.'

He flushed faintly. 'I've annoyed you and that's the last thing I'd ever wish to do, Rose.' He changed the subject quickly to Sue. 'After the hairdresser she'd got a date with some girl friend at the Tudor Rooms in Astead. I thought she said she was due there at eleven but, when I rang just after, she hadn't arrived and as I'd forgotten to ask the girl friend's name it was a bit too involved to leave a message. I didn't want to bother her mother as it's not all that important and she'll be up to the eyes with the VIP lunch she's giving the Member's wife and committee in Cliffhill before the show. I've an idea Sue's planning to drop in here for lunch. She's not a committee member and didn't care for the idea of a solid legal lunch with her old man and myself. But she likes to know my movements and – well – I rather like that, so I keep her in the picture.' He quickened his step as David was circling the Audi. 'How do you like her, David?'

'Very nice. Very nice. What does she do?'

Francis said if he didn't mind the details would wait until he had more time to show the lady off. 'I'm going to be even later for this morning's appointment than I thought.' He held open the front passenger door for me. 'I must know before I go – what the hell's going on up at that inn? Why the chaos?'

'Nothing much,' said David getting into the back. 'Last night the gaffer collected a load of shot in the back of the arm and I nearly got electrocuted in my bath, but aside from that the food's good, beds comfortable, service willing and fellow lodgers amusing in small doses. You and your lovely wife must try it some time, but pack your tranquillizers.'

Francis unclipped the safety-belt he had just put on to twist round and stare at David. 'You're not serious?'

'He is,' I said.

'You mean you really could've been killed?'

'That's right. But for this, that, and more than a little help from my friend Rose. Someone up there,' added David piously, 'must love me and Johnnie Evans-Williams. Let's hope he loves whoever's due for the third.'

'I'd rather not think of that.' Francis was visibly paler. 'Wish to God I hadn't to rush off again.' He turned round, started the car and didn't speak again till he dropped us at the bridge by the inn. 'I'm not normally superstitious, but – er – take care of yourselves.'

I said, 'And you take care on the road to Cliffhill, Francis.

I know you're late but, as old Walt says, better ten minutes late in this world than twenty years too soon in the next.'

He smiled with his lips. 'I wish you'd get that into Sue's head. Cheers.'

I looked after his speeding-up car. 'Trouble with that guy is he's too kind-hearted and has no sense of humour.'

David gazed after the Audi with abstracted eyes. 'Takes all sorts,' he muttered tritely, turned away and walked back to the inn without waiting for me.

4

The yard was bustling with activity. The laundry van was drawn up at the far end by the kitchen entrance; Hilda and the vanman were lifting out baskets and Mrs Evans-Williams was fluttering round tugging her beads. Near the side entrance to the bar, a trapdoor was hooked open, a wooden ramp in place, and Trevor with two hands, Johnnie with one, were rolling up empty barrels and lining them in front of the two open empty garages.

Johnnie stood his barrel upright and advanced on us alternatively to apologize and explode over the standards of modern British workmanship. He was interrupted by Doreen's appearance at the hall entrance. 'You're wanted on the telephone, madam. Mrs Francis Denver. If you'll go along I'll put you through to Box Three.'

David came in with me and noticed a man's suede sheepskin-lined driving coat lying on one low windowsill. 'That's what I need.'

Doreen did a double-take. 'Oh dear. That gentleman with the red car must've left it when he came in to ask for you, madam. He had it slung over one shoulder.'

I paused for a closer look. 'Yes. Looks like Mr Denver's. He's always leaving it around as he never bothers to put it on properly. I'll tell his wife he's forgotten it.'

I had difficulty telling Sue anything. She was ringing from a call-box at the crossroads just beyond Astead woods and was short of change and temper. 'No, darling, don't fuss about ringing back this number. I've got enough if you'll just listen – and don't fuss about that coat. He'll just have to come back for it – no, don't bother to take it this afternoon – just listen! I've had the most maddening morning. Anton took ages over my hair though I told him I'd got a date and had to be out by ten-thirty – '

'Hold on, Sue, and you listen! Francis rang the Tudor just after eleven to tell you he's going to court with your father this afternoon but you hadn't arrived – '

'Of course I hadn't!' She hesitated. 'Actually, as I suppose you've guessed, my date wasn't at the Tudor and I've just waited forty-five minutes in my car and he hasn't turned up!'

'Since when has there been a coffee house outside Astead woods?'

'Darling, don't be thick! Do listen,' she reiterated in her expensive boarding-school whine, 'as I need your help.'

'No! You know what I said last time!'

'Rose, you've got to help me! Actually' – her voice quivered – 'I'm in rather a spot. I just don't dare go to the exhibition – '

'You must! It's your mother's big day.'

'That's why I daren't and you've got to help me. Gordon's got to be there as he wants to flog his pictures and I know if I'm there he'll make a ghastly scene and ruin everything for mummy. He said he would last night. We had a hideous row in his van when he drove me home. He got all hysterical about my leaving Francis, getting a divorce, marrying him – you know what men are like when they're all worked up – and being an artist he takes things so seriously. He doesn't seem to understand we've just been having fun and we have but it wasn't fun last night. So I told him to meet me this morning and talk it out. He knew where in the woods. He's come before on his bike and today he's got the van. He hasn't

come and I know why! He's trying to frighten me and –
well – actually in a way he has as he's got an awful temper.
I can handle him on my own – I can always handle guys
on my own – but not with mummy and everyone around.'

This wasn't the moment so I didn't tell her this moment
had been inevitable for her and the only wonder was that it
hadn't come sooner. 'He could make a scene even if you're
not there.'

'He won't. He'll think I'm sulking because he's just stood
me up and that must mean he's still got me hooked. You
know how conceited men are! They all think they're irresis-
tible. As if I'd leave my home and Francis for a grotty
peasant who can't even raise the price of a gin! I'll handle
him later but I must keep out of his way this afternoon and
you must help me!'

I frowned at my reflection in the box mirror. 'I guess so,
though I still think you're over-dramatizing. Surely if he
wants to flog his pictures he won't start chucking dirt – '

'Won't he just! If he does he'll flog the lot! All mummy's
chums will buy them as conversation-pieces,' she retorted
with rare insight.

'That's true. Okay. What do you want me to say?'

'I've been working it all out in the car and that's what I'll
blame. Actually, I have got a slow in my front nearside, so
I'll drive on to Coxden and get that rather gorgeous guy
opposite the forge to swap it for my spare. It's – oh, God –
it's ten to twelve now – and he shuts up for his dinner hour –
no, that's good, as it means I'll have to wait. I'll have a snack
at the pub there, and after I'll have to wait while he mends
the puncture as daddy makes such a fuss if I only have four
wheels and actually so does Francis. Honestly, sometimes,'
she added peevishly, 'I think cars are the only things Francis
really cares about!'

'So you've said before. You know I don't agree. But you

can't spend the entire afternoon waiting for your slow to be mended.'

'I know that! So I'm going to have one of my headaches and have to go straight home and if Francis is in court that'll work out beautifully! Just sort of tell mummy briefly. She'll be in too much of a tiz-woz about being queen bee and bossing everyone to get in a tiz-woz over me. Tell her I haven't rung her as I didn't want to spoil her lunch party by worrying her and – yes – that I can feel my headache coming on now. Say I'll ring her at home tonight and hope everything is simply super at the show.'

I sighed. 'If I must, but I don't like it and I warn you, this is the last bloody time I'll cover for you!'

'Darling, you're fabulous! What would I do without you? Byeee!' She rang off.

I grimaced at my reflection. Ananias Endel. My God, the messes my married friends got themselves into. Where was the nearest convent? I left the telephone alcove, seething with irritation, and through a hall window saw David checking his car oil. He had added several sweaters beneath his overcoat and looked half a stone heavier. I went outside. 'Do I just call you Nanook of the North?'

'Feel free.' He replaced the dipstick. 'I can't discover why but yesterday she drank oil like it's going out of fashion.'

'Ask them at the garage.'

'Yep.' He glanced at the barrel rollers. 'Our Johnnie's just told me to ask for one Joe Wattle, brother of Harry, who runs it, lives above the shop and doesn't mind being disturbed at his dinner. Best mechanic on the marsh, he says.' He glanced at my face. 'What's Hot Pants been saying to raise your adrenalin?'

'Tell you when we drive over, if I've cooled off.'

'Suit yourself.' He got into his car. 'Back in about half an hour, I imagine.'

'Don't hurry for me.'

He looked at me over his glasses. 'I haven't and I bloody won't,' he added under his breath, and drove off.

The laundry van was just leaving. Johnnie stopped the driver for a word and I was turning to go in when I heard David's car brakes slam on. I swung round. He had gone about a hundred yards up the road to Harbour and had stopped in the middle of the road. I heard Johnnie's 'What the devil – ?' and saw the wisps of black smoke coming from the white bonnet. A second later David had leapt out and was spraying the bonnet with the contents of a small fire-extinguisher. Suddenly, he threw it to one side and charged back towards the bridge. He was nearly there when his car exploded. He pulled off his glasses, flung himself face down on the road and covered the back of his head with his folded arms. A sheet of flame enveloped the car, soared upwards, and the birds rose in outraged clouds.

'Where's the handblocked silk headscarf, Rose?'

I removed one hand from the driving wheel of my Allegro to jerk a thumb at the sling-bag on the back seat. It was a long time since I had been so angry; when very angry I tried to avoid speech.

'Take five,' he said, as if I'd spoken. 'I told you what the insurance bloke said.'

'Just another example of faulty British workmanship?'

'She was French.'

'I'd forgotten that.'

'The insurance bloke said it would teach me to buy British in future, then ruined his plug by listing the new jobs he'd seen go the same way in the last few years. When I explained she'd drunk oil, he reckoned I was better off without her. Engines, he reckons, are like women; get a good 'un and she'll never let you down. Get a bad 'un and she'll never do anything else. Dead lucky, I am, he says.'

'Mention bathrooms?'

'No. His company don't cover me for personal accidents.'

'Are you covered?'

'Yes, of course. By BCC. I told you –'

'You didn't.'

'Yes, before lunch – no – you're right. It was when you were getting tarted up, Johnnie was blowing more fuses, and his lovely wife having her second go of hysterics, and I was knocking back doubles on the house.'

'What did you tell them?'

'That BCC looks after its own, is generous on genuine claims but goes through the evidence with an electronic microscope before parting with sixpence. I said if I'd not got clear the car-insurance bloke wouldn't have been the only bugger sifting through the cold ashes tomorrow and it had to be said that BCC wouldn't be too happy to hear about last night.'

I breathed a little more easily. Only a very little. 'What did Johnnie say?'

'That I was bloody lucky to work for such a good firm.'

'Just call you Lucky Lofthouse?'

'Seeing I've turned accident-prone, more apt than Nanook of the North.'

I said nothing and thought of the scars he would carry on his back and chest for life. Burn scars. In the year before we first met he had spent months in a burns unit after an explosion at work had blown him through the plateglass skylight of his office with his clothes on fire. When he left hospital he had been given six months on full pay and told to find a quiet place by the sea. An advertisement in a Sunday newspaper had resulted in his taking for those months the cottage by Endel's main gate that my late cousin regularly rented to holiday visitors. David had only once talked to me about that explosion; he had never yet talked of his time in the burns unit. I hadn't mentioned it to him and I wasn't doing so now. Only those with no experience of hell suffer from the illusion that there is any therapeutic value in reliving the experience off a psychiatric couch. I knew it was in his mind now. I had seen the old nightmares in his eyes when I raced ahead of the others and reached him as he got to his feet and stared at his blazing car. It was then I had stopped feeling vaguely uneasy and telling myself I was being neurotic and turned very, very angry.

I slowed for the final twist out of Harbour village. The narrow built-up road ahead was the only straight stretch of the route to Cliffhill. I glanced sideways at his calm, unyielding face.

'At least, that's the third.'

He smiled slightly. 'Only thing that finally stopped the poor old girl's hysterics.'

The afternoon was colder, greyer, and on either side and behind us the flat land opened up to the sea on the indented, semicircular horizon. Far ahead the low green hills of the mainland were just visible.

'What did Hot Pants want?'

We both needed a placebo and I knew he could keep his mouth shut. I told him the truth.

'Why bother to cover for her?'

'It's something that's sort of happened. At first I didn't realize it was happening. When I did, I played along, mainly as I like her father and – yes, I like Francis – and though she drives me nuts, I quite like Sue. She is so stupid and so is her mother, but neither can really help that as their men love them being stupid.'

'More than a few do.' He paused. 'What do you know about this Gordon?'

'Very little. I only met him for a few minutes at last year's show. He spent all those minutes leering at Sue and being rude to everyone else. I know he's got digs somewhere in Cliffhill but not why, when he came south, or if he's left a wife and kids behind in Glasgow. He's about thirty and I think working class, so I'd have thought by now he'd have been long married.'

'Working class? He has my sympathy,' he said dryly. 'If Hot Pants fancies herself as Lady Chatterley she rates all she's got coming.'

'You working-class lads have to stick together?' I queried as dryly.

'Why not? What do we owe you toffee-nosed upper-class bastards?'

'For starters, darling,' I drawled, 'the grants that paid for his art school, you at Cambridge and backed your grammar school. It's not the working classes who pay the largest proportion of our taxes and rates, is it? And I'm an ex-grammar bug – '

I glanced at him again and smiled sweetly. 'Up yours, mate.'

He laughed. 'That's why I love you, Rosie.'

'Because I'm an ex-grammar bug?'

'Because behind the cut-glass accent and beautiful, fragile aristo's face, you're the toughest little bitch this side of hell. So he wants to wed her. Doesn't sound as if he's got a wife back home.'

'She says he does.'

'Believe her?'

I hesitated. 'Normally, I never believe anything she says, but on this occasion I think I do. I've never heard her in such a state. It may even do some good. I think it's forced her to realize how fond she is of Francis.'

'And how fond is he of her?'

69

'Very. If not he wouldn't let her push him around. He's not a genuine push-over.'

'No. I'd not have said he was.' He needed more thought. 'How much money has she got?'

'Not a lot yet. She'll have quite a bit when her parents die. Mrs Smith has some of her own and Mr Smith, as he would say, is a man of substance. I've always understood Francis earns good money and I think that must be right as Mr Smith would've gone into that side before they married. Especially as Francis is an incomer and as devoid of relatives as myself. He was raised by an uncle who died when he was in his second year at some northern redbrick. Forget where.'

'How'd they meet?'

'On holiday in Majorca just over four years ago. He moved down here after they married.'

'Why no kids? Pill?'

'Yes.'

We were closer to the mainland and at their southern end the hills had risen and turned into wooded cliffs crowned by the old Norman watchtower and roofs of Cliffhill. It was from that tower that medieval men had watched for the first sign of enemy sails on the sea that had then lapped the foot of those cliffs. Now the flat green land below belonged to the farmers and the birds and lay quiet and drowsy in the soft grey light. The woods climbing the cliffs were alight with autumn; the oaks, golden; chestnuts, crimson; the evergreens, dark emerald shadows; only the elms still wore the green that spilled over on to the slopes beneath the woods and swept on down to the thick ferns and rushes lining the banks of the Marsh Ditch. I slowed almost to a stop before taking the sharp turn off the main marsh road just before it ran on over Coxden bridge. The turn led into the narrower side road that ran parallel with the Ditch north and south of Coxden. In the north the road eventually meandered over another bridge to end at the crossroads beyond Astead woods. The southern arm we were taking ran into Cliffhill.

David twisted round to look at the square Norman tower of Coxden church. 'Looks just as I remember.' He sighed to himself. 'Think Hot Pants has beat it for home now?'

'Expect so. What time is it – oh, no – nearly three. It opened at two. The first bottles of sweet sherry will have long gone.'

'Not sweet?'

'Sorry. Yes. At least, only sweet last year.'

'I shall close my eyes and think of England. It'll make a change,' he said slowly, 'from thinking over your remark last night.'

I stiffened. 'Which one?'

'You know damn well which one. The one that's been in your mind since my car went up. Last night you had Johnnie lined up for the morgue. Now you've swapped names.' He grabbed the wheel. 'Christ, woman, don't have us in the bloody Ditch to prove your point!'

'Sorry – thanks.' I checked the driving mirror fearfully. Luckily, there was nothing behind. I took a deep breath. 'Why – why should anyone be out to get you?'

'I'm thankful to say not even my nasty suspicious mind can come up with that answer. I'm no cop to anyone dead. I've not invented the ultimate deterrent. I don't know any-one who has or any trade secrets that aren't known to every-one in my grade on both sides of the Iron Curtain. Yep, I earn good money – as long as I keep earning. Yep, I've a bit stashed away but no more than'll pay for' – he hesitated – 'that unmentionable car – my next holiday or two and go towards the down payment on the semi-detached I'll have to think of getting when I sell my flat. The lot and my life insurance are tied up to go first to my parents, then my married sister and her four kids. Kids are still in primary school. I can't see any of my family nipping down from Wakefield to do me in for what they may have to come, if they knew it might come their way, which they don't. Apart from my solicitor, you're the only person I've told. Not that the total figure would've put the new roof on Endel. Consequently, I can't come up with one sensible reason why anyone should want me dead. Can you?'

The only reason I could think of made no sense at all while I was alive, nor, from what he had just said, after.

'No,' I said thoughtfully, 'I can't give you one.'

'That's a relief,' he said.

I said nothing.

5

The eighteenth-century town hall stood halfway up Cliff-hill's cobbled high street. The Art Society had taken over the largest assembly hall and by the time we arrived it was packed. The overwhelming number of the Art Soc.'s members were amateurs who made no pretence that their annual exhibition of paintings, etchings, collages, ceramics, pebble jewellery and mobiles was other than a social occasion. It was always a popular occasion on opening afternoon. Attendance by invitation only included 'and guests', free sherry and cheese biscuits.

David impassively surveyed the many middle-aged women with blue hair, too bright lipstick, jersey outfits in muted shades of mud, the few young women in cashmere and tweeds, and the hordes of women of all ages with long straight hair, blackened eyelids, floral smocks or long hand-woven peasant skirts and enough beads and chains strung round their necks to transform Mrs Evans-Williams's seven rows into a model of restraint. The only men visible were resigned, retired husbands or fathers with sherry-flushed faces who knew they were a bit out of touch, what, but couldn't understand what the damned thing was meant to be.

'Australia, all is forgiven. Tell me, love, stands the church clock at ten to three and where the hell's the sherry?'

'If it's the same as last year, up in one of those rooms off the gallery up there.' I looked round. 'I can't see Gordon or any of the handful of professionals who belong to the Soc.

On last year's showing, they've shut themselves up in an upper room with all the bottles and biscuits they can carry and won't emerge till they've run out. But we must find Mrs Smith first – yes – there !'

Mrs Smith's impressive charcoal felt sombrero was outlined against one of the pillars near the ceramics. She spotted me and beckoned authoritatively. 'Rose, have you brought Sue? She's missed the opening !'

'Yes, she's terribly sorry – ' I launched into my set piece. Fortunately, as Sue had forecast, her mother was too preoccupied by, and too much enjoying, her role as a chairman who knew the Member's wife by her first name to be more than superficially concerned. Mrs Smith was a tall, stout woman with the vapid, puffy face of an English rose gone to seed and impeccable dress sense. Her elegant charcoal-and-stone jersey two-piece and exquisite diamond brooch that was her sole ornament diminished in every way the younger, quite pretty and very untidy Member's wife with long strands of black hair floating out from beneath a regrettable purple velvet beret.

'Dear Rose, so thoughtful – poor darling Sue – such a disappointment – she must get her eyes tested. And you've brought Mr Lofthouse !' She had kissed me perfunctorily. She held on to David's hand while she introduced us to her guest of honour. 'We're all simply delighted to have this clever young man amongst us. Simply brilliant, Laura. Splits atoms, and that sort of thing – but you'll know all about that !'

The Member's wife looked suitably knowledgeable on nuclear fission and drew David aside. Mrs Smith returned some of her attention to me. 'Talk to Sue about seeing that new eye man at Astead General. They say he's really quite good even though he's on the Health Service – and she's so fond of you, you'll be able to persuade her. She shouldn't have all these headaches. She was so thrilled last night when she rang to say your friend was back and had driven straight over to Harbour. Now, do tell me – no, I'm not going to ask any indiscreet questions – I merely want to know if you like the inn. Gerald's been quite worried about you as he hadn't time to go over and see for himself. He's been so busy what with all his junior's work and the wretched young man isn't back yet as now his wife and both children have gone down with it. So trying for poor Gerald. I do hope you like the inn as Sue'll be so upset if you don't as it was really her idea.'

'Sue?' I managed to get in. 'But I thought Mr Smith – '

'Of course it was Gerald who made all the arrangements, but at first he wasn't too sure. You know how he likes to take his time thinking things over – but for once he hadn't time. It so happened that, just after having a word with Bill Carmody about you, he had to see one of his junior's clients – I think the client was some friend of Francis or it could be someone he and Sue met at a party – in any event, the client told Gerald he had booked at the inn for his wife and himself but had unexpectedly to go abroad on business and asked Gerald to cancel for him. Gerald immediately thought of your taking it and rang Sue as you young people always know far better than we do what's happening around the marsh. Sue was all for it. She had a word with Francis and he said he'd been quite taken with it when he dropped in occasionally for a drink.' She turned to the others. 'Laura, my dear, I've just been hearing all about Harbour Inn. Rose is having a little rest there. Delightful, she tells me.'

David caught my eye. 'And the food's good.'

The Member's wife said it sounded a real find and she must make a note of the name. 'I'm so sorry to hear your daughter's car – '

'Let her down again and another of her headaches! The poor darling, she'll be so upset as she was so looking forward to seeing you – ah, here comes Nigel Wenden! How nice – you know him, of course? My dear, you must meet him. . . '

David and I removed ourselves to make room for General Wenden's towering figure. The old man sketched a salute my way. 'Rosser's gal, h'mmm? Glad you're off the sick-list.' He marched on.

David took my arm. 'Sherry?'

'Why not? Still can't see Gordon.'

A potter leapt upon us before we were on the gallery stairs. He was about twenty and looked like an ageing pop singer, but he worked in a local arts and crafts shop and knew his public. He had on his old best school suit, a cleanish shirt and tie. The suit was as shiny as his reddened face. He insisted we saw his exhibits, then dismissed his rather good tiles and pots with a shrug. 'One must live, don't ask one why, but one must. What really signifies is one's Future. There! Well?'

His Future was a spindly wooden mobile gallows surrounded by badly made plasticine figures of children, sheep, cows and a few old lead toy soldiers. I hadn't seen anything like it since I left kindergarten.

David and I avoided each other's eyes. 'Very thought-provoking,' he said.

'Precisely my impression, David.'

The potter breathed importantly and half closed his eyes. 'One sensed you two had the inner vision required to appreciate one's intentions. So few, alas, so few.' We all shook our heads sadly. 'What more, one wonders, should one show you?'

I said, 'I found Gordon's pictures very interesting last year. Is he showing today?'

'Gordon? But for Gordon what would this show be? A total in place of semi-travesty. Gordon is the one real creative talent in Cliffhill – all talent – all dedication – he doesn't

76

paint to live, he lives to paint. Starves for it. One can only marvel in humility.'

'National Assistance shut up shop in my absence?' queried David mildly.

I kicked him. 'Where is Gordon?'

'Where, indeed?' Suddenly the potter was near tears. 'One waited in the Fisherman from twenty to one till five to two. He always comes down at one – alas, no sign. One waited outside till the opening was over – one just went on waiting – one sought every inch of this hall – then one just had to retreat for sustenance but one kept popping out – constantly – ' He stood on tiptoe, pirouetted in a circle, then leapt for joy. 'At last! Over there!' He waved both arms ecstatically and charged off.

'One knew,' observed David, 'the US Cavalry wouldn't let one down. Yowl!' He grabbed my hand, lowered his head, hunched his powerful shoulders and bulldozed our path to the potter and the grubby figure in paint-streaked rollneck and jeans backed against another pillar.

Gordon was even thinner than last year, the skin was tight over his high cheekbones and his dark eyes were bruised with fatigue or anxiety, or possibly both. His black hair and fringe beard were neater but his temper hadn't improved. 'Will you stop your blethering,' he was saying belligerently. 'I was working and I forgot the time and why in hell should it matter to you if I did?'

'Hi, Gordon, remember me? Rose.'

He scowled. 'I'd forgotten your name. Not seen you for a wee while.'

'Last year's show. This is David. Had a good year?'

'In this dump? You must be joking.'

'Why stay, then?' asked David.

Gordon was tall enough to see over most heads. His scowling gaze swept the hall as if he expected to find the answer written on one of the walls, or a particular face. 'The light's right and out of season it's dead cheap. Not that you'd think that from this lot.' He raised two fingers. 'This wee man said to wear a suit if I want to flog my pictures. Where'd I get a suit? I can't afford a suit. I've not even the cash for the bare necessities.'

'Like food?'

'Who cares for that? The real necessities. Canvases, paints, frames and the van I've to hire to take my pictures around for flogging. I can't carry them on the back of my Norton.' His scowl was on David. 'Want to see them?'

'That's why we're here.'

Gordon shrugged, did another quick survey around and walked off without bothering to see if we were following. We had lost the potter to a potential customer when we stopped beside Gordon in front of a large canvas covered with bright yellow paint put on with a knife. Just off centre was a large blob in a darker yellow. Gordon folded his arms. 'I've called that one "One".'

David was interested. 'Why?'

Gordon gave David's clean, well-heeled appearance a long, disparaging glance. 'Why waste the time? You'd not understand.'

'Oh, aye? So tha doesn't know t'answer thysel', lad,' retorted David in broad Yorkshire.

Gordon flushed darkly. 'If you're trying to be funny – '

'Come down off that barricade,' said David in his normal voice. 'I asked as I want to know. Why "One"?'

'For God's sake, Gordon,' I put in, 'tell him, or he'll drive us both crazy. He's got no soul, he's a scientist, but he has to know the answers.'

Gordon was unmollified. 'If she's right, what the hell are you doing here, Jimmy?'

'Christ, lad, you've been at the paint pots too long. What

the hell do you think I'm doing here? Trying to lay my hands on Rose's lolly, of course. And her,' he added in afterthought.

Gordon's disarming smile so transformed his face that I suddenly glimpsed what had attracted Sue. It interested me, but the attraction was missing. 'Is that a fact?'

'Yep. Why "One"?'

'I couldn't think what else to call it. This one's "Two".'

'Two' was yellow with a red blob; in 'Three' the blob was orange and in the top left corner; in 'Four', white and mid-centre. 'What do you think?'

David shook his head. 'I don't as I don't understand them.'

Gordon was gloomily delighted. 'What'd I say? Then you'll not want to buy one.'

David's kick stopped my wasting thirty pounds. 'No,' he said, 'no. They wouldn't like Endel House where Rose lives and I'm without fixed address. Be sheer cruelty to hang those on four-hundred-year-old walls, to walls and them.'

'Your man's right.' Gordon turned on me eagerly. 'I'd forgotten you were from Endel. Are you not a girl friend of – of Susie Denver?'

'Sure. My neighbour. I've just been telling her mother why she hasn't arrived – ' I repeated my piece and added the invention, 'I didn't want to worry Mrs Smith but I shouldn't be surprised if Sue's getting flu. This bug going round starts with a crashing headache. I know. I've just had it.'

He was so relieved he beamed. 'You could be right. Susie was here yesterday getting this place ready and she was a wee bit – a wee bit – '

'Off-colour?' I suggested unoriginally.

'Aye, you could say that. She'll not be coming?'

'I'm afraid not.'

'Gordon, thank heavens I've found you! I've been looking everywhere!' A small fair girl with blackened eyelids
and clinking neckchains had thrust her way through and
grabbed his arm. 'Please come, please! You're the only
person Ivor listens to and the way he's hung my Leda you
can't see the Swan for Marcella's bloody pots! Do come
– please!' She hauled him away.

David muttered weakly, 'Get up them stairs, Rose. Booze
or you'll carry me out feet first.'

'Hope there's some left.'

'Dregs'll be nectar after over-exposure to young love
unrequited.'

'Love? You think he is serious?'

'I think he thinks he is. She could be doing right to stay
away,' he said on the stairs. 'For my money she's got him
to boiling-point and God only knows what any emotionally
disturbed nut won't do at that temperature.'

'Nut?'

'What bloke in his right mind spends hours bunging blobs
on paint and then asking thirty quid for them? You were
another nut to think of wasting good money and don't tell
me you'll not miss it. That wasn't why. You were sorry for
him. Weren't you?'

I coloured. 'Show that much?'

'Yep. And to him. A nut but no fool. Kick a bloke below
the belt if you must and your aim's good, but don't kick his
professional integrity. If our Gordon were open to handouts
he'd not look as if he only eats once a week and he doesn't
drink 'em either. He hasn't the eyes of a boozer. He fancies
his blobs and would rather go hungry than flog 'em to those
who don't see them as he does. As blobs they might even be
good. I wouldn't know. I hope so for his sake.'

I turned at the top to look down over the gallery rail at
the black head above the crowd. 'Just call me Ananias.'

'You mean Sapphira.'

'So I do. I'd forgotten.'

'I know you have,' he said curtly. 'I haven't. I need booze.'

'Just a moment.' I watched a tall, distinguished grey-haired man who had just come in, making purposefully for the taller figure of General Wenden. I recognized the first man though he was out of uniform as he was another of my father's boyhood friends who labelled me 'Rosser's gal'. 'Look. There's the Chief Constable. Remember him?'

David glanced down casually. 'Yep. He a culture vulture?'

'I wouldn't have said so. Of course, he lives in Coxden and his wife and Mrs Smith are huge buddies. Lady Hurst's a member – yes – there she is over by the collages. Blue pudding-basin hat. She must've press-ganged him along. We'd better look at those collages. She's always making them.'

'Booze first.'

It was about an hour later, after we had shared the remains of the last bottle with other late arrivals and worked our way round the exhibits to end a few yards from the exit, that General Wenden stopped me.

'Off, Rose?'

'Yes, general. Most impressive show.' I introduced David. 'I don't think you met David,' I added, 'when he and I stayed with your brother and sister-in-law just after Endel's roof gave. Weren't you in Hong Kong with your son and daughter-in-law?'

'I was. Interesting spot.' The general's six foot five made David look slight. 'Yes.' He studied David keenly. 'Remember my sister-in-law mentioning you, Lofthouse. You two in a hurry or care for a cup of tea first? They do quite a decent tea at the Wheatsheaf.'

David said politely, 'Thanks. sir. We're in no hurry.'

81

I said, 'I can't see Mrs Smith but we should say good-bye – '

The general didn't seem to hear. He took my arm and marched me out. I was rather relieved. I could ring Mrs Smith later and preferred that to more evasions about now. Also, I was curious. General Wenden had no daughters, his wife had died many years ago, and he always seemed to me a man who preferred a womanless existence, not for the obvious reason, but because he regarded women as a strange species that made him feel uneasy. He and I had never yet had any conversation that lasted more than two minutes and concerned much more than the weather and his roses. He had retired some time in the fifties to a small house in Shepland, his home village, that was maintained for him by his former batman and batman's wife with the military neatness with which he maintained his garden. He was a passionate gardener and grew the best roses on the marsh.

The Wheatsheaf was further up the high street on the same side as the town hall. The general ushered us to an empty table in one bay window, beckoned the aged waiter, ordered tea, and announced it was good gardening weather.

I said, 'It was good of you to leave your garden for the show. I didn't know you were a member, general.'

'I'm not. M'wife was. Kept up her subscription. Believe in supporting local enterprises.' The thick grey eyebrows met over severe blue eyes. 'You a member, Rose?'

'I'm afraid not. And – well – David's just here on holiday.'

'Don't make excuses for him, gal. He looks well able to stand up for himself. You've been in the sun, Lofthouse. Where?'

David was watching the general keenly. He discussed Australia with the old man until out tea arrived, I'd been instructed to pour, and the bread and butter, jam and scones had been arranged to the general's liking.

'Glad you're here,' said the general. 'Gather you're an old friend of young Rose's, h'mmm?'

'Yes, sir.' David hesitated, then astonished me by asking quietly, 'Am I right in thinking you've some bad news to give her?'

'Very astute. Like an astute fellow. Regrettably, yes. Wanted you sitting down first, Rose. A woman needs to sit down and have a cup of tea on these occasions.'

I put down my cup, looked at David, then the old, lined, teak face, and saw the sadness in the faded blue eyes and suddenly felt very cold. 'Tell me straight, please, general.'

He looked about to ensure no one else was within hearing. 'Very well, m'dear. Nasty business, I fear. Poor young Susan Denver's body was pulled out of the Ditch ten miles north of Coxden bridge just under two hours ago. Lady Hurst has taken Mrs Smith back to her home to wait until Gerald Smith can leave court and take her home to Astead. They had to get Francis Denver out of court to identify his wife's body. Not that there was any doubt, but routine, h'mmm! She doesn't seem to have been in the water more than a couple of hours at the most.'

Too stunned for speech, I just stared at him.

David reached for one of my hands. 'I presume you know how she got in the Ditch, sir?'

'H'mmm. Yes. Her car skidded across the road and hit an ash on the bank, then bounced off. The driver's door was jolted open on impact, she was flung out. From the state of the car she was going much too fast for that bit of road. Nasty bit of road. Nasty twist where the Ditch bends sharp south. No witnesses. Wouldn't expect any this time of the year and especially not on Astead market day. All the local farmers'll be in Astead and don't generally start for home until the pubs close for the afternoon. Poor gal was driving alone and not wearing her safety-belt. Seems to have hit the back of her head a nasty smack. Wearing some sort of a leather hat they say, but nothing strong enough to cushion the blow. They've fished out the hat. Poor gal seems to have been dead before she hit the water, and from the marks on the rushes rolled down the bank. Very nasty business. Very sad. Pretty young thing. No sense, but pretty young thing. Always drove too fast. Used to see her. Probably be alive now if she'd worn her safety-belt. Great blow to her husband and parents. Very sad.'

I turned away and stared at the cobbles of the high street. 'No,' I said mechanically, 'she never remembered to wear her safety-belt.'

As if from a long way away I heard David's 'Was it the car roof that got her head?'

And the general's 'From the marks on the hat and the tree – the tree. Difficult to be sure yet. She was still wearing the hat when Charlie Gillon spotted her body floating face downwards when he was driving his tractor back to Shepland from Coxden. I imagine the poor gal was on her way here.'

'No.' I turned back to the two men. 'She rang me at about twelve. She said she had a slow and was making for Coxden garage.' I was about to say more when I saw the expression in David's eyes.

It was then I remembered that this morning Sue had been to the hairdresser.

6

We stayed in the Wheatsheaf after the general left and moved first to the bar, then the dining room. Our dinner looked good. I'd no idea how it tasted and nor, from his abstracted expression, had David.

Over coffee, I said abruptly, 'Walt Ames and me.'

'Come again?'

'Walt says he can smell danger like he can smell strangers. I'm not so hot on strangers but I've just realized I can smell danger. I smelt it yesterday just after saying good-bye to Sue. It never occurred to me to associate it with her, so first I rationalized it as my being *persona non grata*, then I pinned it on Johnnie, then you. I was crazy and so were you. Nothing to do with old ghosts or your coming back into my life.' He was eyeing me speculatively. 'Just something in the present.'

'Oh, aye? Then why're you still looking like you don't fancy the smell in here?'

I looked around the rather elegant little dining room. It wasn't crowded but the tables on either side of ours were occupied and the tables were close together. I didn't recognize any of our fellow diners but as it was out of season they were unlikely to be visitors to the district. 'Later.'

He nodded and emptied our wine bottle into my glass. He was driving us back.

'You said earlier you wanted to ring the Smiths before we left. That still on?'

I sighed. 'I dread it but I must. They should've been

85

home some time now. I expect Dr Carmody's driven up from St Martin's and given her a sedative but Mr Smith'll still be up. He's helped me so much.'

'Would you prefer to drive over to Astead? I can wait in the car.'

'Thanks, but no. I'd feel an intruder tonight. I'm not a relative and, should Mrs Smith be up, it could add to the agony seeing me alive when Sue's dead. Mightn't be so bad for her if she liked me. She doesn't.'

'No. I saw that this afternoon.'

I smiled wryly. 'I'd forgotten your talent for getting relationships right at sight.'

The talent didn't seem to amuse him. He frowned into his coffee cup. 'How about Francis?'

'I shouldn't think he'll want to talk or see anyone tonight. I'll do something about him tomorrow – and I'm dreading that too. I feel so – well – responsible –'

'Don't be a bloody moron, woman! By no strength of imagination can you be blamed –'

'It mightn't have happened if I'd not played along –'

'Balls. She'd have done what she wanted to do with or without your help. Didn't she always?' I shrugged. 'You know damn well she did. If you're going to make that call, get it over and let's get going. There's a public phone in the foyer. Got enough change?'

I nodded vaguely. My mind had gone back to Sue this morning and was giving me the impression that something she had said would have struck me as odd had I not been so irritated. I couldn't remember what it was. I stood up. 'Don't expect I'll be long.'

I wasn't. It merely seemed so.

I went back to David. 'He was sweet and so sad: His wife's in bed under sedation. Francis has gone home alone and says he's taking his phone off the hook and not answering the doorbell till morning. Oh dear. Why, why, if it had to happen, did it have to happen on Mrs Smith's gala afternoon?'

He gave me a long blank look. 'That's just what I've been thinking. Let's go.'

'Has he brought our bill?'

'Yep,' he snapped, 'and if you're thinking of handing me your share, bloody think again or I'll make the scene to beat all.'

I looked at his face and believed him. 'Thank you very much.'

'Don't thank me for my inhibiting Nonconformist upbringing,' was all he said until we were about three miles from Coxden bridge and on the road by the Ditch.

'Spell it out, Rose.'

'It'll probably convince you I'm a nutter.'

'It won't as you're not one, even though you sometimes act like one. I know you're not and so do the genuine nutters and that's why they latch on to you like limpets. They need your strength and you're generally fool enough to let them have it as you're fool enough to feel sorry for them. That's why you married one nutter and will probably end up marrying another. Spell it out!'

The night was as dark as this morning before dawn, now we had left the lights of Cliffhill behind. The sky was hidden by high, slowly moving clouds, and the marsh was shrouded in black. Our headlights split the darkness like searchlights and made the road glisten, and silvered the bank rushes and caught the disembodied jewelled eyes of frightened rabbits and the black oily surface of the deadly water.

'David, it's that hat. I can't understand why she had on that hat.'

He didn't turn his face from the windscreen but I saw his shadowed outline stiffen. 'Why can't you?'

'She'd just come from the hairdresser. It was a fine windless morning. Maybe someone her mother's age might've put on a headscarf or even a hairnet after the drier. Not Sue. She loathed headscarves and only wore a hat in the rain. The idea of her flattening her new hairdo with a tight hot suede hat just doesn't make sense.'

'You said she was steamed-up. People do odd things when they are. Couldn't she have forgotten her hair and just shoved it on?'

'Sue? Forget her appearance? Only over her – ' I broke off. About a minute later, I said, 'Her looks were the big thing in her life.'

'One of the two big things.'

I winced. 'Hell, she's dead. Skip the porn.'

'I'm not recalling it for laughs. I'm just stating the fundamental cause of her death. If poor little Hot Pants hadn't had 'em, she wouldn't now be a stiff on a morgue shelf. She'd be home with hubby, he'd be putting the cat out and saying how about bed, and that poor sod Gordon would be slapping out another blob for posterity. Instead, I'll bet Francis is now well into his first bottle of whisky and Gordon well into his second.'

'Gin,' I corrected mechanically.

'How do you know that?'

It took me a few seconds to remember. 'Sue was griping this morning about his not being able to afford gin. Must've been his gin. She only drank wine. Spirits give a girl bags under the eyes.'

'That's for sure. Gordon must've been south longer than I assumed.'

I didn't want to think of Gordon. I had to. We had reached Coxden bridge. Astead crossroads were only just under twelve miles off and beyond the crossroads were the three miles of Astead woods. I waited until we had turned on to the main marsh road. 'Charles always forgot the time when he was writing. I suppose artists do when they're painting.'

'Like hell you think Gordon forgot the time. You were so sure what he was doing in his lunch hour you nearly had old Wenden tipping off his chum the Chief Constable to dispatch a couple of lads in raincoats to ask him to give them a hand with their inquiries.'

'Hence your dirty look?'

'Personally,' he said dryly, 'I believe in doing a bit of thinking before I suggest sending someone up for a life stretch. Admittedly, I hadn't then seen your point about the hairdresser or realized you'd gone on to the question, who put the hat on for her. You had, hadn't you?'

'Yes.'

'Why was it put on?'

'Huh?'

'Why put it on her head?'

'How – how do I know?'

'No. It is a problem. I haven't come up with the answer either.'

'Come?' I felt both sick and relieved. It was a nasty combination. 'Been bugging you too?'

He nodded. 'Nearly as much as the clout that seems to have killed her. I've been reminding myself we got it third-hand from an old boy who got it second and might've got it wrong, though I doubt that.'

'He's on the ball.'

'So I thought.'

'And he seemed quite sure it was just an accident and that that's how the cops see it.'

'Yep. The cops' view is important. The ordinary cops mayn't be forensic experts, but by God they're experts at fishing bodies out of dykes down here and picking up the pieces after road accidents everywhere. They're first on the spot and their first impressions of what caused the spot are right more often than not. At the same time, if they do have reasons for doubt, they don't commit themselves until they've had their pathologist's PM report. If this one's satisfactory, once Gordon's dried off, he can get on with his blobs.'

'Oh, God, David, I hope it is.' He was silent. 'Now you spell it out, man! Why do you think that crack on the back of the head wouldn't have killed her?'

'I didn't say it wouldn't, or couldn't. I'm just surprised that (a) it didn't knock off her hat, and (b) that she wasn't dead before she hit the tree. I know there's no limit to the types of fatal injuries anyone can collect when flung out of a car crashing at speed, but as she was driving and not wearing a seat belt, I'd have expected her first to collect what's known in the accident trade as a windscreen fracture and whiplash.'

It took all my self-control to try to pretend we were discussing accidents academically. Without the pretence I couldn't do it. 'You mean she should've been pitched forward, not sideways?'

'Yes.' He flattened a hand over the front of his head. 'This is usually what hits the windscreen, gets an instant fracture and the force whips back the head and breaks the neck. The whiplash.'

'How do you know all this?'

He hesitated and I understood why directly he began speaking. 'That burns unit I was in, was in a hospital near a motorway junction. It had a large accident unit. Once I was allowed up and to potter more or less where I pleased, I used to drink coffee and chat up the accident staff in their breathing spells. Medics and nurses never talk anything but shop. Bits rubbed off on me.' He jerked his head my way. 'They used to call the seat you're in the suicide seat. Not all that many seat-belts around four years ago.'

'No.'

He was briefly silent. Then, 'What's Gordon's surname?'

'No idea. Could be Gordon. That's how he signs his pictures.'

'I saw that. That bloke has problems, but, as I said, no fool. If, after she rang you, he had nipped out from behind a tree, clouted her one, shoved on her hat for some reason of his own, fixed the car to look like a crash and then beat it back to Cliffhill, I'd have thought he'd enough nous to horse straight into the Fisherman for a lunchtime booze with chummy.'

'You also said there was no saying what any emotionally disturbed nut at boiling-point would do.'

'Trust Lofthouse to open his big mouth too wide.'

'Why the sackcloth? I'd have said that was fair comment.'

'Maybe. I was still daft to make it. It's the kind of daft comment people make when they're letting themselves get carried away by some unproven theory that just happens to suit their ideas at that moment. We're doing that now. If we don't slam on the brakes, we'll soon be hanging Johnnie's arm, my bathroom and my car on Gordon. Whatever he was or wasn't doing before he showed up this afternoon, from what Sue herself told you, last evening he wasn't going berserk with a shotgun or a screwdriver in Harbour, he was driving her back to St Martin's having a bloody row.'

'No,' I protested, 'no! Don't confuse me now I've finally agreed with you that the goings-on at Harbour have all been genuine accidents. The inn's got no connection with Sue – ' I stopped abruptly. 'I wonder why she was so keen for me to stay there?'

'Was she?'

I told him what Mrs Smith had said, then answered myself. 'Maybe she thought she could use my spare bed as an alibi for staying out overnight. She'd tried that one on me at Endel. Couple of times when Francis has been abroad she'd even tried suggesting she brought her current love to Endel. I wouldn't buy either. I told her Endel was my home not a brothel. She got hellish narked.'

'Nothing like the truth for raising the hackles.' From his tone his mind had gone off on a frolic of its own. We had gone a few more miles before he came back. 'I think we should cool this till we hear the PM report. If it's straight-forward, that'll be at the inquest, if not, we'll hear sooner than most. You're probably the last person she spoke to alive. Knowing your bush-telegraph, old Wenden'll have passed that on already.'

'Yes. Oh God. If the cops ask me about that call they'll want to know what she said.'

'Not necessarily. They may just want to know the time to keep their books straight. Don't waste sweat until you have to.'

'Thanks.' I relaxed slightly. 'I was getting carried away again.' I looked thoughtfully at his solid profile. 'You'll probably want to slug me for this, as I know how men love and cherish their new cars and I'm terribly sorry about yours, but I don't mind telling you I'm glad you'll have to stay put a few more days till the replacement arrives. I wouldn't much fancy this set-up on my own.'

'I wouldn't much fancy your dealing with it on your own, though I haven't the least doubt you'd manage very well. But thanks for soothing my ego. It can use it.'

We drove on in our first companionable silence since his return.

There was very little traffic on the marsh and when we reached the straight stretch to Harbour village we had the road to ourselves. We had gone about half a mile when our headlights picked up the red rear reflector on a lightless motorbike hitched on its stand so near the left edge of the road that the shadowy figure crouched between bike and dyke bank barely had footroom.

David slowed the car. 'Looks just a kid with a broken-down bike, but take a good look round.'

I did. 'I can't see anyone else about and there's nowhere safe to hide. Water on both sides and the banks slippery as hell.'

'Don't remind me.' He drew up about fifteen feet from the bike. 'Keep your door locked, get into this seat when I get out, keep her running, in gear, and your foot on the clutch. If I walk into anything don't try and rescue me. Beat it like hell for the Harbour cop.'

'All right,' I lied to save argument.

David got out. 'What's up with your bike?'

The figure had straightened and was blinking suspiciously in our lights. It was a slight youthful figure in shiny black jacket and jeans with long damp dark curls hanging round a thin fine-boned face made garishly white by the lights. I only recognized it was a boy when he spoke. 'You don't need to bother. She got a leak and gone dry. Just taking a look before I push her home. I lives down Harbour.' He flattened a hand to protect his eyes, peered more keenly at the car and exclaimed, 'I know that job! I seen it one of the gar-ridges down the inn. That's the young lady from Endel's Allegro. She back there? You from the inn?' He peered at David. 'I don't know you.'

'I don't know you, lad. Leak? Let's see. No point in giving you a transfusion that'll run straight out.'

I looked more closely at the boy's face then got out. 'Mike!'

The boy's head swung round. 'How'd you know me name?'

'I think I met your father last night. Harry Wattle.'

'I'm Mike Wattle.'

I switched off the engine and joined them. 'I thought you must be.'

He looked me up and down. 'You the one as owns Endel?' I nodded. 'Cor! Me dad says you got more land than anyone down the marsh. You're a proper little 'un for that lot, aren't you?'

I looked him up and down. He was about five foot seven. I quoted Walt Ames, 'Smaller we are better we float.'

Mike grinned. 'Me dad says that.'

'Now we have security clearance,' said David, 'why do you think your job's got a leak? I can't feel one.'

' 'Cause she gone dry, mister. She shouldn't never. She gone lovely all day, same as always. After me work she takes me over to me bird Coxden way. Her dad's got this farm two miles our side. She starts back lovely, then up the road here she splutters and stops. Dry, she is. She shouldn't never be!'

David investigated the main and emergency petrol tanks. 'Dry as they come. How long've you been riding her?'

'Since I passed me test straight off October last year. Why?'

'Why, you daft ha'porth? After that time you should know to the yard what she'll do to the mile.'

' 'Course I know!' Mike's pride was outraged. 'Forty she does for all she's an old job and carries the two in her main and the half in her emergency. She was full right up when I start this morning and I only done the seventy-two today. Does the hundred nicely when she's full. I know as she was full this morning as me Uncle Joe he filled her right up last night after me dad gone spare and sends me home for saying as I see that Mrs le Vere's fancy man back the dunes after the guv'nor – ' He heard himself and stopped in horror. 'I didn't ought to have said that – me dad'll skin me alive he will – none of your business he says – oh I didn't ought to have said – '

'Cool it, lad,' said David kindly. 'We've got bad hearing and worse memories. So you should have twenty-eight miles left?' Mike nodded unhappily. 'Must be a leak. Or did anyone borrow this job today?'

'Not – oh yes! But she'll not have done more than six. That Mrs le Vere – she borrows it when we stops for the dinner-break down Lymchurch way to nip into Lymchurch to fetch the stomach tablets for Mr le Vere. He gets this indigestion, see. Always has a few tablets in his tin but when he looks dinner-time he's not got none left and me dad says as they have them up the post office stores Lymchurch and Mrs le Vere says if I'll lend her me bike she'll fetch 'em. Often borrows me bike dinner-times to do a bit of shopping when we stops near a village, she does. Used to last year. Fancies a bit of shopping she does, seemly.' He smiled foxily and jerked a thumb at the helmet hanging from the handlebars. 'Borrows me skid-lid and me jackets. Fancies herself in me gear, she does, but that Mr le Vere was real made-up when she come back with the new tablets as his stomach was playing up nasty and that Dr McCabe he don't have no stomach tablets in the box he has with the syringe and needle and the stuff for Mr le Vere's diabetes case he gets took real queer whiles we're out, but he hasn't never been took queer. Not the once,' he added regretfully.

'You can't win 'em all, lad. Got a tube handy? Let's see what happens when we transfuse. You don't mind losing a little petrol, Rose?'

'Of course not. Help yourselves.'

Mike beamed. 'Thanks, miss. I got me tube in here.' He rootled in his toolbox, thrust aside a collection of rags, odd gloves, a couple of scarves, hauled out a long piece of tubing, then held up one scarf to the light. It was pale-blue wool.

'That's not mine nor me bird's – oh yes! That Mrs le Vere had it on this morning. She must've taken it off dinner-time and forgotten.'

I said, 'If you like I'll return it for you, Mike.' He handed it over. I went back to the car and put the scarf in my sling-bag with my still unused handblocked silk, while they shifted the bike up to my petrol tank.

'I'll suck it up, mister. Got me spit in it already.' Mike inserted one end of the tube into my tank, sucked, spat petrol, and yelped with joy as the flow ran smoothly. 'She's off.' He looked at David with new interest. 'You staying down the inn?'

'Yes. Arrived yesterday.'

'You did? Oh, yes, I know who you are! You're the one with the new French job as gone up this morning. Never seen nothing like it he hasn't, the guv'nor tells me dad and me when we fetches 'em back. Wonder he wasn't fried, he says. What she want to do that for?'

'I'm not sure. My guess is, a combination of faulty wiring and petrol leak. I can't find one here. That the lot? Right. We'll keep behind you into Harbour in case she's fooling us. Take it easy. The lady doesn't like driving fast and nor do I. Give her a kick.' The bike roared to life. 'Sounds healthy. On your way, lad.'

'Thanks, mister,' yelled Mike happily, 'thanks ever so. And you, miss.' He roared off with more noise than speed.

David got back into the car. 'Three mechanical faults. Tidy world you live in, love.'

'So it appears.'

He glanced at me without further comment. We stayed silent while we followed Mike into Harbour. He drew up outside one in a row of cottages, jerked both thumbs in the air and waved us off with shouts of 'Going lovely! Thanks ever so! 'Night!'

The Anchor was still open, but Harbour village rose early and went to bed early and the single, winding village street was deserted. The lights were on behind the closed curtains of the upper windows, and most of the ground floors were in darkness. The small, squat, grey stone cottages and the few slightly larger houses were all crouched with their backs to the sea and their dark, slate, windowless roofs sweeping down to within a couple of feet of the back doors. And all looked to have grown out of, rather than been built on, their muddy mounds. The village was too small and too isolated to be commuter territory, and the few weekenders or retired towns-folk who managed to move in seldom stayed more than one winter. It was not xenophobia that drove them out; it was the wind, the mists, and the mud that from November to late March transformed the neatest gardens into a morass.

The lights were out in Joe Wattle's petrol pumps and in the post-office-cum-general-store, but shone intact in the telephone box on the pavement outside. In a village where everyone knew everyone else and few owned private telephones, potential telephone vandals knew they had no hope of escaping detection and instant retribution, not from the law, but from parents, grandparents, uncles, aunts and neighbours.

'Never seen a marsh village before, Rose?'

'Just wondering where fancy man lives. Obviously, local.'

'Unless our Angie's free with the hush money. I'd say she'd need to be, whatever he is. Her old man may realize he's only got himself to blame for marrying a woman who could be his daughter, but if he caught her at it I doubt he'd hesitate to divorce her. He's done it once. They say divorce is like murder. Only the first that sticks in the throat and then it becomes a habit. I don't see Angie exchanging a solid citizen who bears all the hallmarks of being a good provider for any simple village lad.'

I thought uneasily of Sue. 'No. Nor me. Though Renny has the odd weakness.'

'She knew that when she married him. She was no wide-eyed virgin and nor was he. I'll lay a year's pay,' he mused, 'that while he's happy for the little woman to enjoy the fleshpots while he can enjoy them, he's taken good care she'll never be a wealthy widow and knows it. He'll leave his all to his daughters. No flies on old Renny. He likes to take good care of his health.'

'Even to the extent of bringing his tame medic on hols. As you guessed last night.'

'Wasn't much of a problem. Angie was being so blatantly patronizing, and Linda so blatantly resenting it, that obviously there had to be a good reason for their taking their hols together. Commonest things being the most common, the reason was either money or sex. I kept an open mind till I took a look at Nick McCabe. He fancies his wife and likes shooting. Ergo, Renny's footing their bill and why not, if he can afford it?'

I thought about this. It made a restful change. 'Yes. I'm sure you're right. Linda can't stick Angie but she's sticking it out for Nick's sake. She's hooked on him. Isn't it a relief to meet a married couple who actually love each other.'

'I've known more than a few that do. Could be as so much of my life was spent amongst people with just enough to keep the rent-book straight providing the grocer'll leave it on the slate for another week. You need money and time to waste both on fancy men or fancy women, and not many men in our street had that and none of the women. It was only when I moved up that I discovered both were as common a hobby as golf amongst the better-heeled. Or is that one of my chips showing?'

'No. From what I've seen of my married chums here and when I was married, you're dead right again.'

We had left the lights of Harbour behind and directly ahead and all around was darkness lit only by the approaching lights of the inn. I felt they should have been welcoming but, possibly as they looked so lonely, the sensation they gave me wasn't one I welcomed.

'David.'

'Yep?'

'Perhaps fancy man was just aiming at a duck when he accidentally got Johnnie.'

'If it was fancy man who pulled that specific trigger.'

'Must've been, surely? Mike and me dad are sure of it.'

'Mike and me dad are sure I'm your fancy man. If they can be wrong once why not twice. If they're not wrong twice, yes, I agree. Somewhere on this marsh there's one bloody lucky duck.' He crawled the car over the last bridge and into the yard. 'And right now, love,' he added unemotionally, 'I know just how that feathered bugger feels.'

7

Mrs Evans-Williams welcomed us as if we were back from South America. She had exchanged her multicoloureds for five rows of mock-jet beads and, from the way her hand reached for them every time she mentioned anything connected with David's car, she was wearing them in mourning for its demise. She didn't touch them when she said his bathroom had been temporarily repaired by Biggs of Cliffhill and was quite safe for what she delicately termed normal purposes, but dear Johnnie would be happier if the bath remained unused until the whole ceiling was taken down and reconstructed. 'Perhaps you wouldn't mind using the staff bathroom in the attic, Mr Lofthouse?'

I said, 'He can borrow my bath if you don't object.'

'So kind – ' She ducked into the office to pull out and push in a couple of plugs in the small switchboard, listen momentarily to one of the headphone earpieces, then ducked back. 'Just Angie ringing off. Had a lovely outing?'

David said the exhibition had been interesting and we'd dined at the Wheatsheaf.

'How delightful. Good food?'

'Yes, thanks. So my insurance bloke comes out at ten tomorrow? Good. And how's your husband tonight?'

'A little tired and sore but dear Nick says that's only to be expected and has managed to persuade him to have an early night. We've had a really peaceful evening as everyone's a little tired after the best day out yet! You should see the cold store – can't turn round! So nice for them all.' She smiled indulgently at the four farmers propping up the bar watching Trevor refill their pints in a contented bleary silence. 'The McCabes are watching some special late documentary on television, the others are in the lounge and if you'd care for coffee or any other hot drink Trevor can slip out for it. Harry should be back any moment. He's sleeping in again – such a comfort. Would you care for anything?'

'Not for me, thanks. I'd like to go straight up. How about you, David?'

He glanced at the farmers. 'I think I'll have a nightcap in there first. Would you care to join me in one, Mrs Evans-Williams?'

That evoked one of her girlish giggles. 'How kind – I'd love to but I don't think I should. No head at all. One sniff of a barmaid's apron and I'm woozy! But thank you so much, Mr Lofthouse – so kind.'

'Sweeties, you're back!' Angie sailed out of the residents' corridor with both arms outstretched. She had topped her black velvet pants with a scarlet sweater and looked vividly attractive and even happier than in the yard last night. 'Sweeties, we've had the most fabulous day! Absolutely exhausting but fabulous! Just everything went right – what am I saying?' She slapped a hand over her mouth and flapped her eyelashes at David. 'Do forgive me, sweetie! I am the world's most tactless woman and I never remember things – but your car – your poor car – and whatever it was that happened to your bath – the blood froze! It absolutely froze! Have you always been accident-prone?'

'Personally, my dear,' drawled Renny, ambling after her, 'as I said earlier, I think the dear boy was born lucky. Good to see you back, dear people. I hope you'll both join us for a final drink before we push on up. I'm allowing myself one extra tonight as we really have had a splendid day's shooting, if a trifle long for yours truly. Anno Domini catching up, alas.'

David said quickly, 'I was just hoping you'd join me, I dislike drinking alone and Rose is opting out. She's – er – rather upset,' he paused deliberately, 'for a reason I know she'd prefer me to explain in her absence.'

I was glad to get away but puzzled by his method of arranging this. When it came to handing out gratuitous information on personal matters, David normally had much in common with Mr Smith. I heard the low murmur of his voice but not what he was saying, as I went up the stairs. I was on the landing when I heard the mock-jets hitting the floor like machine-gun fire. I glanced down. David and Renny were on their knees picking up beads, Mrs Evans-Williams with eyes popping was clutching her bare neck and Angie was exclaiming dramatically, 'I knew it! I knew it! Didn't I tell you, Renny, sweetie, something ghastly would have to happen to a third person?'

I was undressed, in my kaftan, and about to run a bath when I remembered her scarf. I cursed and took it out of my bag. I was in no mood to go down again tonight. I shook the scarf free of creases to refold it properly, looked at it more closely and carefully picked off a few strands that weren't blue wool. I held them in the palm of my hand, looked at them for a few moments, then went over to my anorak that was hanging on the back of the door, dug in both pockets and took out the messy collection of mohair I had picked up in the nethouse. The purple and green strands from the scarf were identical. I realized there was a possibility the scarf had picked them up in Mike's toolbox but, probably as Sue was so much on my mind, I was sure they had come off the fodder. Sue would have thought a roll in a nethouse rather gorgeous. Angie, absolutely fabulous. Sue had stopped overworking 'fabulous' some time last year. And then I remembered she had used it this morning, and David's remark about people doing odd things when steamed-up. Was that what had niggled me at dinner?

I sat in an armchair to think. I was still there when David knocked softly a good hour later. He looked surprised by the speed with which I unlocked the door. 'From the silence I thought you'd dropped off with the light on.'

'Just brooding. Come in a minute.' I closed the door, showed him the mohair and explained. 'He's local. Only locals know about nethouses. Good wake?'

'I've known better though I had it for free. How to make friends and influence people. Miss death the odd time and have a good gory tale to tell.'

'Why were you so keen to tell it? And shove me out first?'

He said gently, 'I thought I might as well get it over and stop them bombarding you with questions. They were bound to hear from the helps in the morning. I only beat the Mc-Cabes by a short head. There was a bit about it on the local late-night news. Nick remembered the name from your conversation with Renny last night. They came charging into the bar with the tidings. Have you finished with your bath or shall I come back?'

'Have it now. And, thanks.'

'Any time. Right.' He paused and seemed about to say something, then changed his mind. He went for his things and after a very quick bath, paused again and smoothed down his damp pale-gold hair. 'Gordon?'

'Yes. I can't get rid of the feeling that she was murdered.' He looked at me in silence. 'You think so too or you'd have slapped that down.'

'What I think right now is that you need a sleeping tablet. Got any?'

'No. I hate 'em.'

'So do I, but there are times when we all have to do things

we hate and this is one. I haven't any. I'm going to knock on McCabe's door. What's the use of a doctor in the house if you don't use him?'

'David, no, you mustn't bother him – '

'Stuff that. Why else did he take the Hippocratic oath?' He vanished before I could protest further and was back with Nick McCabe in less than a minute.

Nick was sweet. 'Why, surely, Rose, I appreciate you require a little help with sedation for one night. You have had a kind of real traumatic experience.' He opened his neat medical case and hesitated over his decision before taking out a bottle of capsules. 'If you are not accustomed to nocturnal medication I guess just the one of these will suffice, but I'll leave you the two.'

David was interested in the contents of the case. 'You've come prepared to deal with most things.'

'I would not say that. I merely have the basics such as insulin, adrenalin, morphine, cardiac stimulants and so forth.' He studied me clinically. 'You look real tuckered out tonight, Rose. You'll feel a lot better after a good sleep – oh, Linda said to tell you she is real sorry but will not mention this to you as we both surely appreciate you will not care to talk about your friend. I have been in Britain the five years and having married with a Britisher I guess I have come to understand your British reserve. Not that it was too hard for me as my parents were both from Scotland – down the Lowlands – and folk do not come much more reserved than from those parts. Okay now? Have a real good sleep.'

David held out a glass of water. 'Knock it back as the doctor says, Rosie. That's it.'

'David, you're a hideous bully.'

He grinned, 'Sleep well.' He went out with Nick.

I went out like a light directly I got into bed and the next thing I knew was Doreen shaking me. It was half past eight, my tea was getting cold, and I was wanted on the telephone. 'Sorry to wake you again, madam, but Mrs Evans-Williams said she was sure you'd not mind going down in your dressing-gown as there's no one around now they've all gone shooting and it's that poor gentleman as lost his poor wife in the Ditch yesterday afternoon – and the turn that gives me when Mrs Evans-Williams says as she was a friend of yours – never, I says, not that poor young lady as been poorly – here you are, madam, and your slippers. . . .'

'Thanks, Doreen.' I tore down the corridor rubbing my eyes and was only half awake when I reached the alcove and went into the wrong box.

'Never mind,' said Mrs Evans-Williams's breathless voice. 'I'll change over – through now.'

'Thanks. Francis? Rose.'

'I've woken you – but I had to. I've been walking the marsh for hours and' – he was trying to steady his voice – 'I just had to talk to someone who understands and I know you will. Can I come over and see you? I've got to come over to collect that damned coat I forgot yesterday – and there's so much I've got to do – but I must see you. Can I come?'

There was only one answer. 'Of course. Do you want to come to breakfast?'

'My God, I can't eat!'

'I know you don't want to but you must. Please.'

'If you say so I'll have something here. I've got so many calls I've got to make – about ten? Too earl, ?"

'Any time'll suit. Francis, I am so sorry –'

'I know – don't say any more – ' He slammed down his receiver.

The log fire in the lounge had stopped spitting and the heap of uncleared white ash below the iron basket glowed red when Hilda came in with our coffee. It was closer to eleven than ten when Francis arrived. David had long disappeared in his insurance man's car to look over the remains in Joe Wattle's backyard. Hilda's chubby face was unnaturally solemn. She moved on tiptoe and spoke in a whisper. Old English tribal customs died as hard on the marsh as in the rest of the country. She eyed Francis covertly and approved of his drawn, white face, black tie and the dark-grey business suit he had told me he had on for the Smiths' sake as they had insisted he lunch with them.

I put his coffee at his elbow. 'I know you're trying to chuck smoking,' I said when Hilda closed the door behind her as if it were thistledown, 'but if you've got any on you, have one. If not I'll get you a packet from one of the machines in the bar.'

'I've been chaining all night.' He produced a squashed packet and wasted two matches before he was able to light the cigarette. 'I knew you'd understand.' He inhaled deeply. 'I've been thinking in the night – all night – that you're just about the one person I know who can understand how I feel at this moment. That's why I had to come to you.' He paused as if he were having to haul each word from his battered mind and had to be sure it was the right one before he voiced it. 'I want to tell you why. You – you won't like it and – and I won't like saying it – but I must – I must be honest with someone and I know you'll understand. Can you bear it?'

He was my friend and neighbour and I'd been engrained with old English tribal customs. 'You say anything you want to say, Fancis.'

His strained dark-blue eyes appraised me unhappily. 'First I want to say how much I've always admired your loyalty to your husband. I've never heard you say one unkind word about him or about your marriage, though – though I've always suspected it wasn't happy. No, please – I'm not going to ask questions – I just wanted you to know – I've known and understood your attitude and – and shared it more than you've ever known.' He saw the expression that flickered through my eyes before I could stop it. 'I'm not blind, Rose,' he said in a harsh tone I'd never heard him use before, 'and like you I married for love. And in one way I'll always remember Susie with love though I've known – my God, have I not known – for years – that she wasn't the girl I had thought I married. You knew that too.' He caught my hands with both his and his hands were icy. 'Don't turn away! Don't try and pretend any more. It's too damn late. You can't hurt her now and I know she often upset – no, saddened – you as much as she hurt me. I know that as surely as I know that when you married – like me – when you said for better or for worse, you bloody meant it.' He dropped my hands, got up, roamed the room, then swung round, savagely. 'Know what you and I are? Couple of crazy anachronisms! Believing in marriage vows! Huh! How olde worlde can you get? And you did, didn't you?'

I felt as if I had been kicked in the chest. I just nodded.

'And didn't you keep hoping one day – somehow – one day – things would work out? That one day you'd be able to stop pretending to yourself – not merely to the world – to yourself?' I nodded again. 'My God, Rose, don't I understand! Haven't I had to pretend to myself – but I had to! I loved her. God, how I loved her and – yes – yes – I know she was fond of me but she never loved me as I loved her and don't you now dare to pretend she did!' He spat the words. 'You're so kind, but don't you dare try and be kind to me about that now! Different for her parents and they're another reason why I had to keep on pretending. I – I bloody like my father-in-law tremendously. I wish he were my real father. I mightn't if I could remember mine but I can't. And though my mother-in-law is one of the most infuriatingly silly women I've come across, she means well and she's been good to me and she – and he – so adored Susie and were so proud of her. How could I hurt them?'

I had never liked him so much as I did at that moment, and yet, strangely, I felt as if I was with a stranger. He neither looked nor sounded the man I had known as Sue's husband. It was as if the cellophane wrapping had suddenly been ripped off exposing the genuine article beneath. 'You couldn't hurt them, Francis. You've been a marvellous son-in-law, and I've got to say it, a marvellous husband. Never forget that. Whatever else you think you must forget, never forget that.'

'I did try – ' His voice cracked, he covered his eyes with one hand and turned away. He walked to the far end of the lounge and stood hunched over one of the glass cases with his shaking shoulders towards me. I was glad for his sake that he had the relief of tears, even though, after what he had just said, I was a little surprised he still had tears to shed. He had touched so many of my old scars that I couldn't avoid remembering how I had shed so many tears in marriage that, when it was abruptly ended by a plane crash, my eyes had run dry.

Eventually, I went over to him. 'Come and sit down now and have that coffee.'

He gave a long shuddering sigh, turned, put both hands on my shoulders. 'Yes. Thanks.' His voice was calm and beneath the reddened eyelids his eyes had calmed. 'I need it – and you – to help me pick up the pieces. You will, won't you?'

'Of course.'

'God bless you, my dear.' He bent his head and gently kissed my cheek. 'I was feeling so alone. You don't know what it means to know you're – ' He broke off and jerked up his head as the door was quickly closed behind us.

I glanced round. 'Hilda back?'

'Hilda – ?' He was frowning. 'The maid? No. I'm not sure who it was. Some chap in outdoor clothes. Gone too soon to see who.'

'Probably David back from Harbour as I don't think more than the staff are around.' I took him back to the sofa and, to give him time to get himself back in control, told him about David's car.

He was aghast. 'Went up? Just like that? Why?'

'Not sure. David thinks probably a combination of faulty wiring and a petrol leak.'

'He should know. With his knowledge of electronics there can't be much he doesn't know about wiring. In fact – God – what am I thinking? I must be crazy!'

I was curious. 'What were you about to say?'

He shook his head. 'Quite crazy. Forget it. Just thinking aloud.'

'What were you thinking? Tell me. I want to know.'

He hesitated, then with obvious reluctance said, 'Well, it suddenly occurred to me that – er – well – if any chap should know how to fix a machine to do – er – well – anything – well – he should.'

I gaped. 'You're not suggesting he'd blow up his new car? For God's sake, why?'

'Don't look at me like that! You mustn't be angry with me. I'm too shot to pieces to know what I'm saying and you did insist. I don't know the answers to anything this morning. It's just that as yesterday you'd given me the impression you'd given him another thumbs down and he looked as sold on you as he's always been – and – and – I suddenly thought having no car would give him an alibi for hanging on down here.'

I was very angry but managed to batten it down as I was sorry for him. 'Duckie,' I said gently, 'if David wanted an excuse for staying on, to send up his car in flames would be the last he'd use. He might not have got clear in time. He's already gone up in flames once. His back and chest are covered in scars and I've seen 'em.'

He flushed to the roots of his dark-red hair. 'I – I'd no idea. When?'

'Four years ago.'

He averted his face and gazed into the fire until the pallor returned to his tense face. 'The year Susie and I married.' He blinked furiously. 'Her mother told me this morning she rang you yesterday. You – you must've been the last person she spoke to.'

'Yes.' I prayed he wouldn't ask what she had said. My prayer must've been heard.

'Was this long after I'd gone?'

'No. A few minutes later. About a quarter to twelve.'

He nodded vaguely. 'I'd stopped to fill up in Harbour just about then. I know as the chap at the garage was just telling some woman she'd missed the eleven-forty bus into Cliffhill and I gave her a lift. Chatty woman. Talked non-stop. Can't remember what she said or who she was.' He looked at his watch. 'I'll have to go. I don't want to be late for lunch. My mother-in-law gets in such a tiz about meals. And I've got to call in on the Astead police first. Just routine details, the chap said.'

I looked into the fire. 'I'm afraid it is routine for them.'

'That's what the chap said,' he repeated.

I stood up and picked up his driving coat. 'Don't forget this.'

'No. I can come back and see you here, can't I?'

Again I saw no alternative. 'Of course.'

There was no one around in the hall or yard when I saw him off. I was thinking about police routine and noticed one of the doors of the three garages that had previously been open and empty was now shut. When I got back in, Mrs

Evans-Williams had reappeared and was fussing over the books on the counter. She told me David had asked her to tell me he was back and in his room writing letters and that the le Veres had decided to come back for lunch and have a quiet afternoon. 'Pity you'll not be in as they'd have enjoyed your company. Your packed lunches are ready for whenever you want them.'

The packed lunches were news to me. Welcome news. I felt far too emotionally mangled for Angie le Vere's overpowering artificiality. I murmured something trite about it being a nice day for a picnic.

'As Mr Lofthouse said when he asked for the packed lunches. And I think' – for once she stopped dithering and her pinched face was extraordinarily sympathetic – 'he feels you need a little bit of peace. As dear Johnnie was just saying, you came to us to rest and really you've had so little.'

I let that go and asked after Johnnie.

'Much better, thank you. He had a splendid night and a really good lie-in this morning. I put my foot down. Don't you dare cross that yard, I said, until lunchtime. But I mustn't keep you as you're going out – oh, yes, please tell Mr Lofthouse not to trouble to let us know about dinner. As you're residents, if you are too late for the main serving we can arrange something to suit you.'

I said truthfully that was nice to know as I wasn't sure of our plans for the rest of the day.

I went slowly up the stairs and along the passage. Angie came out of her room as I reached the door and clearly hadn't heard me. Before she did the quick change, from her expression she had walked out of the room in a blazing temper. 'Sweetie, hallo!' She smiled widely with her lips. 'Renny's a bit fagged so we've decided to skip the sporting life for the rest of the day.'

'Renny,' announced Renny's voice from the room, 'is using his intelligence for once.' She held back the door for me to see him lying under a rug on a bed, reading a paperback. He lowered the book and pushed his glasses on to his forehead. 'The time has come for old Johnnie and I to accept we're a couple of old crocks due for the chimney corner.'

I smiled at him. 'With every respect, Renny, 1 d say that any old crocks who can be out from dawn to dusk for days on end, outshoot everyone around and only need the odd half-day off before getting back into the action, won't be due for the chimney corner for at least another thirty years.'

His heavy, fleshy, mottled face creased in a charming smile. 'Dear lovely little lady, thank you kindly for your kind words. How well I understand why young Einstein has rushed back twelve thousand miles to be at your side. Kindness in a woman' – he glanced at his wife – 'is much more rare than rubies.'

Angie flicked back her hair defiantly. 'It's no use bitching at me because I'm hopeless with sick people, Renny. If you wanted a nurse you should've married one. You knew all I knew about was acting – and don't tell me I was lousy at it as I know it!'

I wasn't going to stand on the sideline while they fought it out. Before Renny could answer, I told Angie I had one of her scarves and how I'd come by it. 'Mike Wattle seems a nice kid.'

'An absolute sweetie!'

'Pleasant. Solid wood between the ears, but pleasant,' Renny allowed. 'Run dry, eh?'

'Unless he found the leak after we left him.'

'Doubt it, as he was on his machine at dawn this morning.' Renny replaced his glasses, picked up his book and studied the pages intently, probably as he was holding them upside-down.

Angie came with me for her scarf but, fortunately, didn't linger. She flapped her eyelashes at the twin beds. 'You are a clever little sweetie. Saves so. much trauma and chat, separate rooms. Bless you for salvaging this scarf. I adore it. See you at luch.'

'I'm afraid not. We're having a picnic.'

That smile reached her eyes. 'How fabulous for you both! See you!'

I waited a minute or so, then knocked on David's door. 'Not locked, Rose. Come in,' he called.

I opened the door. 'How'd you know it was me?'

He wasn't writing letters. He was lying on his bed blowing smoke rings. 'Forgotten my gun-dog ears?'

'Yes.' I leant against the door. 'You forgot to tell me we're off on a picnic.'

'Didn't forget. No chance. Any objections?'

'None. All for it.'

He got off the bed. 'Hellish as that?'

'Worse.'

'Wept on your shoulder?'

'Metaphorically, though it mayn't have looked like that to you.'

He was puzzled. 'Why to me?'

'Didn't you look in and back out smartly?'

He shook his head. 'Haven't been near the lounge since my bloke ran me back. The Audi was still outside. I didn't think my busting in on the scene would help either of you so I came up here. After asking for our lunches.'

'Clever of you to guess I'd want out.'

'Didn't take much intelligence to guess he'd pull out all the emotional stops and what that would do to you or anyone else with a front seat in the stalls. It's only the non-English who think the English unemotional and there's nothing like sudden death for ripping off the lid.'

'Ain't that the truth. Must've been Renny. Francis said some man.' I drifted over to the room's one window, looked out on the marsh, and was glad it had been Renny. He wasn't emotionally involved with me and being an experienced middle-aged man he'd know that at such moments such things tended to happen and a few moments later to be forgotten. 'What did your insurance man say after seeing it?'

'Very much what he said yesterday. One variation. He can't get a replacement inside of a week.'

'Come back to Endel when we leave here.'

'Let's deal with that later.' He joined me at the window. 'Where shall we picnic?'

We could see the sea over the wall. The tide was going out, the sand appearing and glittering in the bright sunshine. I didn't want to look at one dyke, but I loved looking at the sea. 'Have you any idea where Harry's taken the guns today?'

'Yes. Renny said same spot as yesterday as it was such good value.'

I grimaced. 'Not for the ducks. Anyway, that's nor'-east. That's the Harbour Wall down there. Sou'-east. Let's just nip down in the car and take ourselves over it on to the beach. Or do you hate looking at the sea?'

'Suits me, so long as we get one thing straight first. No paddling. I'm not having my feet drop off from frost-bite.'

'Deal. Paddling's out.' I opened the window and leant out to scan the marsh. 'So are all those threatened poachers, from the serenity of the birds. They've got the place to themselves like yesterday morning. Not, as I said from the start, that I'd expect to see any around in daylight.' I shut the window. 'Have you noticed how everyone here seems to have lost interest in poachers since Johnnie was shot?'

He had removed his jacket to add a couple of sweaters.

He surfaced red-faced. 'They have had one or two other things on their mind,' he observed mildly. 'Wish I'd me long-johns.'

I laughed. 'I could lend you some tights if you can get your size elevens into them.' I made for the door. 'Don't forget the woolly muffler and spare socks.'

'For that you don't borrow me balaclava.'

We left the car in a parking place against the sea wall and climbed the steep narrow concrete steps on the inland side. It was a glorious autumn rather than November day, and even on top of the wall there was a breeze no stronger than the flapping of gentle wings. From up there the outline of the old harbour was especially clear. The unusual warmth of the sun had raised a faint haze about a foot high over the low land between the stranded arms. 'The ghost of the lost sea back again,' said David. 'Long time since I've seen that. Think we're in for a mist tonight?'

'I'd say that haze'll go when the sun goes.' I turned to the sea. 'The tide can't go much further out and the turn may bring in a change of weather.'

The steps running down to the beach were nearly as sand-papered as the slanting stretch of pebbles that banked the wall and were washed clean at high tide. Beyond the pebbles a silvery band of sand roughly 200 yards wide curved the isthmus. We were at the centre of the indent and on either side the land formed two ends of a shallow horseshoe, then curved away. Beyond the curves and out of our sight, the wall was much further from the sea and between the beach proper and wall were the dunes tufted with sea-grass and reeds. There were very few rocks off Harbour, and those few were only visible at low water and were no longer considered dangers to shipping. It was the sea that was the danger, because of the hidden power of the cross- and under-currents.

The sea was at peace with the land that day. The water was a soft clear grey, lazily lapping the sand. The gulls jostled for footroom on the handful of rocks and ranged the lengths of the two massive terracotta pipes running out from beneath the wall and over pebbles and sand into the sea. The pipes were the outlets of the dykes in Harbour Marsh and wide enough to swallow with ease the body of a sheep, or a big man, and wash the body out to sea either for eternity, or until, and often weeks later, it was returned unrecognizable by some incoming tide.

After we had lunched against the wall, David turned down his overcoat collar. 'Warm for the first time since I set foot on beautiful broken-down Britain,' he murmured sleepily. He settled himself more comfortably, folded his arms, closed his eyes, and from his quiet breathing was asleep almost immediately. I kept an eye on his unguarded face as he had forgotten to take off his glasses, and noticed how, even when relaxed, his face remained quite disconcertingly intelligent and solidly sensible. Of course, Francis didn't know him well and Francis had been right off-balance. Nevertheless Francis was intelligent; how, after one look at David's face, could anyone with intelligence imagine David would be stupid enough to risk his life, or serious injuries, just to give him an excuse to stay at the inn a few more days? Had Francis known David as well as I did, he'd have known David could take, and once had taken, a calculated risk on his own life to save mine and won the gamble. If he had to, he'd do that again for me or anyone else. Not for anything less. How could Francis – ? Then I had to remember he hadn't known what he was saying or doing this morning – and I hadn't known him, at all.

Odd, that sensation that he was stranger. Worse than odd to think of Sue this time yesterday.

I stared at the gulls on one drain. I didn't see them. I was seeing the great main outlet of the Ditch at Norharbour, the seaside town on the tip of the mainland just opposite the extreme north-east tip of the marsh. If Sue's body had not been found so quickly, within hours it would have sunk into the slime at the bottom and then, eventually, it would have been carried down the Ditch through the outlet that ran far out into the sea. Would Gordon know that? Almost certainly. I knew he had lived in Cliffhill at least a year and it was common local knowledge that the Ditch drained out at Norharbour like a young river and had the widest outlet of the marsh.

'What's up with the smell, Rose.'

I started. 'Thought you were asleep.'

'Just thinking. I do it best with eyes shut.'

'Like me sketching. I wish I'd brought a block.'

'Oh, aye?' He felt into his pockets and produced the block, sketches and pencils I'd dropped yesterday. 'You name it, Lofthouse has it.' He looked at the sketches. 'These are damn good.'

'Not really. I'm not being modest. Take a better look and you'll see they're more caricatures than sketches. I can see a likeness because I can caricature. That's what's fooling you.'

'I didn't know you could caricature. Do faces?'

'Sometimes. Some come off, some don't. I used to do them at school to the joy of my form and rage of the art master.'

'Do me.' He struck a pose. 'While I'm holding still, as a *quid pro quo* you can tell me what's on your mind.'

I didn't need to look at his face as I had it in mind. I concentrated on the block. 'Mainly, Francis this morning.'

'Uh-huh? What did he say that's dug deep?'

I told him all but one item.

'So he'd caught on? Can't say I'm surprised. I've never thought him a fool.'

I glanced up. 'Would you've put up with it?'

'No. Not even from you. Turning the other cheek isn't one of my kicks. First one and I'd pack my bags for good. But I've never fancied the life of a pseud country gentleman. For those that do, it seems a good life. He fancies it more than a bit, doesn't he?'

'I've always thought so. But I've always thought he was too hooked on Sue to know what time it is.'

He grinned. 'Don't let it throw you, love. You always were a bloody awful judge of a bloke. Let's see that one. Hey! You are good! But I can't have a jaw that size.'

I considered this and shook my head. 'No. Yours is bigger.'

'I'll ignore that as I'm hellish impressed. I'd no idea you'd this talent.'

I sniffed. 'I'm not just a pretty face.'

'I'll say you're not! Think of all that lovely lolly. Do another – Francis. You've just done me without one look so you can do him from memory as you've just see him.'

'I'll try.' A couple of minutes later I stopped drawing. 'No. I've gone wrong. I'm making him look like Johnnie.'

He looked over my shoulder. 'You are, rather. Shove on a moustache for fun – go on.'

'Right.' I shaded it in, then smiled. 'Daft. I must've had Johnnie in mind.' I pulled off the page and was about to rip it in half when he took it from me. 'Why do you want it?'

'Amuses me. I'm easily amused. Do Renny.'

'Half a minute.' The gulls had caught my attention. A cloud was hovering over what seemed a long dark shadow floating at the distant water's edge. 'What's that down there?' I stood up for a better look. 'See those gulls over something being washed ashore?'

He gazed with narrowed eyes. 'Too far for my short sight. I can just see a kind of shadow. Probably a cloud.'

'There aren't any.' I walked further down the pebbles. 'It

looks – oh God!' I caught my breath, sharply. 'David! I
think it's a body being washed up – ' I raced down the
pebbles on to the sand. I had gone about a hundred yards
when I heard him shouting. I didn't bother to glance or stop.
I could now see clearly the long dark object floating just
under the water that seemed wrapped in a dark blanket.
I was so sure that it was a body that for some irrational
reason I must save from the sea that I forgot where I was and
the dangers of running on untested sand anywhere on that
coast. I remembered both facts less than five seconds later.
In those seconds my wellingtons sank to their turned-down
tops and I couldn't get either out. I didn't use too much
force on the effort. My common sense had belatedly returned
and my immediate reaction was more fury than fear. Everyone said there were no longer quicksands off Harbour. Everyone hadn't told the birds. It was then I noticed there wasn't
one on the patch of sand around me.

David's shouts made my head twist back. 'Keep off!' I
yelled. 'I'm on quicksand!'

He was racing towards me. 'I know you are, moron!
Keep still and don't struggle!'

'I'm not! I'm just trying to get out of my boots. I'm not
sinking fast – maybe I'll hit rock soon. Don't come nearer!'

He had slowed down and began putting one foot carefully
in front of the other. He was about six feet away when his
front foot suddenly sunk. He hauled it out by flinging himself backwards and even saved his shoe. He leapt up, pulled
off his overcoat, looked swiftly around for driftwood. There
was none about. 'We'll manage with this,' he said calmly.
'Just grab what you can when I fling. I'll hang on to this
end.'

The sand was trickling over the top of my boots and
seeping into my trouser legs, and I was very frightened. I
could feel panic rising in waves and gripping my throat.

Each wave rose higher and each grip was tighter. I had to lick my lips to answer. 'Sure.'

'Easy does it, love. Here she comes!'

It was the fourth attempt and my boots had vanished when I caught one sleeve.

It only took minutes. Years had seemed shorter. When the final heave catapulted me free and face down over the sand, he hauled me clear and toppled backwards and we fell in a heap, gasping like stranded fishes. Despite the physical effort, his face was white under the sweat, sand and tan, and for a few seconds we just stared at each other in agonized relief. 'Thanks,' I muttered breathlessly, 'thanks very much.'

He didn't say anything. He stood up jerkily, slung the sand-sodden overcoat over one shoulder, picked me up in his arms, carried me back to our picnic place and dumped me down as if I were a sack of potatoes. He dropped on to the pebbles beside me, leant back against the wall breathing painfully, took off his glasses and cleaned off the sand. He had replaced them when he observed dryly, 'As of now, your ancestors are known as the Revolving Endels.'

Suddenly euphoric with the triumph of being alive, I shouted with laughter. 'God, yes! I don't know what happened to my Endel blood! If Walt Ames ever hears this I'll never hear the end of it. But, hell, everyone always says there aren't quicksands off Harbour.'

'No one ever tell you quicksands are known as shifting sands because the buggers are always shifting?' He held out a hand and I took it. His hand was much colder than mine. 'Forty-eight hours with you and I'm turning into an old man. I haven't your talent or stamina for living dangerously.' His grip tightened. 'I thought I was losing you for good. For the first time since we met I was glad you've never fancied me. If you'd been my young and lovely wife, the Sunday papers would've had themselves a bonus.'

'Oh, no! I'd forgotten!' Memory wiped the smile off my face. 'Yes, you would've been in rather a spot.'

He let go of my hand, hitched down his glasses and looked at me very keenly. 'What had you forgotten?'

He had saved my life twice. The shock was hitting me. I couldn't act. I told him the truth and saw his face harden. 'If you're going to start taking umbrage. David – cool it! I've no relatives. You have. Parents, sister, nieces and nephews. If you don't want to use it, shove it on to them. In any event, if you die before me, they get it. Mr Smith's got it all tied up.'

'Oh, aye?' He lit a cigarette. 'He approve?'

'No. Purely because he's sure I'll change my mind, marry again, have kids, continue the entail.'

'He could be right.'

'No.'

He was still watching me keenly. 'So you've said. And he said not to tell me in case I was tempted to do you in for it?'

I met his eyes. 'He said that even although from my account you had proven yourself the most trustworthy of young men, where large sums of money were concerned as a matter of principle he never trusted anyone. He also said it would be most unfair to you to raise expectations that events might prove to be unjustified.'

'Good points, both. Who else knows?'

'Just him and me, and now you. He drew up the will himself. When he got in his junior partner to witness my signature with him, he covered all but the signature spaces with a piece of foolscap. After the junior left, while I was there, he locked the will in my strong-box, locked that in his office safe. Only he knows the combination. He says when he dies they'll have to blow the lock but that way he'll probably die more peacefully.' It was an incredible relief to have this in the open. 'He won't have told anyone. I haven't. That's why in the car yesterday I couldn't give you one sensible reason for anyone wanting you rubbed out. Thank God.'

'That figures, but you don't. I know how you've rationalized this to yourself, but it's still daft. Why me? Nothing but picture postcards for over two years and then this turn-up for the book. If you're wanting thanks, too bloody bad, as I don't bloody want Endel.'

'Then it's just as well you've stuck around to keep me alive, mate, or you'd have bloody got it twenty minutes ago! Oh – that body!' I would have jumped up had he not lunged sideways and held me down with both hands. 'David, we forgot – '

'Belt up, listen and look! Down there! Even I can see it clearly now. It's no body. It's some old rug someone's forgotten. Floating under the water opened out like a magic carpet.'

'How can I see anything in this half-nelson?' I pushed him off without difficulty and saw the wide squarish dark patch floating in with the turned tide. The sea was nearing the quicksand. 'If it did hold a body, that's dropped.' I began pulling off my filthy socks, rolling up my filthy trouser legs. 'Soon as it's safe, I'm fishing it out.'

' "Deal," she said. "No paddling," she said.'

'So I've changed my mind. Mr Smith says that is a feminine prerogative no woman of his experience has ever allowed to fall into disuse. I'm not asking you to paddle. I'm just curious to know exactly what it was that very nearly had me killing myself.'

He leant back against the wall, refolded his arms, half closed his eyes and spoke with his cigarette dangling from one corner of his mouth. 'Will you please tell the jury, Dr Lofthouse,' he drawled in an Oxbridge accent, 'if you were aware that the late Mrs Rose Mary Douglas, *née* Endel, had named you as her sole heir before she entered the sea on that tragic occasion? You were so aware! Indeed. And you have just told us that this unfortunate woman had only a matter of twenty minutes or so earlier managed, with your assistance, to free herself from a patch of quicksand. You have told us it was a fine afternoon, but in early November. I put it to you, Dr Lofthouse, that in early November the English Channel is too cold for sea-bathing. You would agree? I'm greatly obliged. Yet you insist the unfortunate young woman was determined to paddle and you were unable to prevent her. Would you object to my describing you as a strong, healthy man in the prime of life, Dr Lofthouse? No? I'm greatly obliged. Would you be so good as to tell the jury your height? Just under six foot. Indeed. And your weight? Approximately thirteen stones. Now I have here the pathologist's report that states the late Mrs Rose Mary Douglas, *née* Endel, was twenty-six years old, five foot three inches in height and weighed seven stones. Yet you say you were unable to prevent her taking this rash action – may I remind you, Dr Lofthouse, you are under oath?' He removed and stubbed out his cigarette. 'With luck and good behaviour I might be out in five years but your lot'll have gone to the crown. You don't collect when you inherit by foul play,' he added in his own voice.

I mopped my streaming eyes. 'I expect the Duchy of Lancaster can use a little help.' I removed the rest of the sand from my face, then pulled out a comb and did my hair. 'Don't forget to tell the jury I've tidied myself. That'll make any woman on it certain it wasn't suicide.'

He was laughing too. 'When I tell them I've paddled with you, they'll exchange the five years for probation and psychiatric treatment.' He was removing his shoes and socks. 'This'll teach me to make deals with women.'

'No one has asked you to paddle. Anyway, you don't have to freeze your feet yet. Sea's not high enough.'

'I want to make bloody sure all feeling's dead before they drop off in the water. I've got to come in with you. My neck goes with your neck and I'm fussy about my neck.'

'Not always.'

He went scarlet. 'What the hell – ' he began as if he had genuinely forgotten that night three years ago. 'Stuff that one, or I'll get nasty. When I get nasty I play dirty and as I've just told the jury I'm a lot bigger than you and this is one very lonely beach.'

'Okay.' I turned my attention to the floating object and again leapt up. 'David. It is a rug and – and I think I can see the colours. Let's go closer.'

We walked down hand in hand and were too interested to remember our freezing feet. We couldn't be sure until we dragged the soaking rug from the sea. Then we were so sure we didn't say anything as we wrung it out between us, carried it up and spread it out on the pebbles. The purple and green plaid pattern of the mohair had been washed free of sand and slime but apparently it had not been in long enough for the water to remove the dyke reeds threaded and twisted through the material, or the largish darkish stain splayed over the middle of one end and the two smaller similar patches on either side.

I sat back on my feet and watched his fair head bending over the middle stain. 'The rug's in good condition. Why drop it in a dyke? Or do you think it fell off the back of fancy man's motorbike – if he has one? Or she slung it to him to catch when they left the nethouse, he missed and it fell into the cross-dyke? Or vice versa?'

'Not knowing can't say.' He sat on his heels. 'That's not oil. It could be that he got himself a duck after all and wrapped it in this when he made his getaway.'

'Yeuk! You think that's duck blood?' Then I remembered something and had to shake my head. 'No self-respecting marshman would throw away a good rug just because it got splashed with bird blood. The pockets of poachers' jackets are usually stiff with old dried blood and so are shooting jackets. Walt's got one that can practically stand up by itself and smells revolting.' I examined the largest stain again. 'You sure it's blood? Couldn't it be rust?'

'Possibly. Depends how long it's been in the sea. If it is blood I'd have expected the salt to shift it, though when this sort of material gets impregnated it'll take longer to shift.' He had another peer, then looked straight up at me. 'If this is duck blood I think you're right. Must've fallen into a dyke accidentally.' His tone was as empty of expression as his face but the computer was flicking over at maximum speed.

'What do you really think it is?'

'What I really think,' he said, 'is that I'd like to take a look in that nethouse.'

I was suddenly aware that my feet and I were very, very cold.

8

'Nasty dangerous habit, smoking.' David crouched among the cold ashes that were all that remained of the fodder on the nethouse floor, and lit a cigarette. 'Put down your fag one moment and the next you're dialling 999.'

I sat gingerly on my feet that were now encased in the aged pair of spare wellingtons that with four sacks and a spade lived in my car boot from September to April. The sacks now encased the wet mohair rug. The fire seemed to have driven out or killed all the spiders, but about spiders I took no chances. 'Drop one in stuff as dry as this was yesterday and it'd have gone up in a couple of minutes. Hardly any smoke.'

'Particularly if the door was shut.' He crawled over to examine the inside of the door. 'Yes. Charred by flame. Come out of there, Rose. I only wanted another look at that fungus. And the joint pongs of worse than burnt offerings.'

I didn't query that last. I followed him out. 'Another look? Did you see it yesterday?'

'Not properly. I just noticed a kind of greenish glint and, like you, thought it was natural growth.' He brushed ash and sand off himself while looking searchingly at the ground round our feet and over the strip of sandy grass between the footpath and cross-dyke. 'Next time you take me on a picnic I'm wearing me full protective clobber.'

'Shove in a handy Geiger counter as well.' I walked nearer the dyke for a closer inspection of the grass. 'Yes.

Ash here – here – and there. He came down to wash his boots.'

'Or she.' He lunged for me. 'Come away from those rushes.'

'All right. I've done enough paddling for one day.'

'You still haven't done your stint of walking on water.' He drew my arm through his and patted my hand. 'Kindly remember (a) my neck and (b) we're in full view of the inn.'

'I'd forgotten that.' I looked towards the inn and then at his quiet face and thought aloud. 'Nothing like sex for a good cover story. It's the one everyone'll believe as it's the one everyone wants to believe.'

He nodded vaguely. 'Let's get going.'

The short afternoon was dying fast and the sun a great red ball just touching the marsh that had lost its warmth. The land was turning sepia, the dyke water a lifeless dark brown, the birds were beginning to settle for the night, but the frogs were wide awake and so was the sea. In the west the clear sky was pinkish grey; in the east it was heavy with dark clouds that had come up with the tide. We had left the beach well before the water reached the pebbles and it was now growling softly against the wall. We walked back to the car and my mind went back to walking that same path with Francis yesterday. It seemed a lifetime away, and it was.

Trevor, oozing efficiency in a black jacket over his porter's waistcoat, was running the inn. 'Got to face it, the missus she's not as young as she was and it's been all go all week so she gone over the flat for a bit of a kip and the guv'nor he's driven into Astead with that Mrs le Vere. Albert's out back, but he don't fancy the hall as he can't get the hang of the switchboard only he don't like to say – and a right twist he'd have been in just after the missus and the guv'nor gone what with that Mr le Vere wanting to be put through to the one daughter in Aberdeen and the other in Brussels and then

127

his office in London. Would you like your teas now? Albert'll fetch them into the lounge for you.'

'Not just yet thanks. Baths, first.'

He smirked knowingly. 'Yea. Picked up a bit of sand haven't you – oh – you'll pardon me – all go like as I says –' He bustled back to the switchboard.

David and I exchanged glances, I went up alone, he went back to the car for the sack-wrapped rug we had originally decided to leave in the boot until tonight. 'Easier now,' he said when he came up with it under the overcoat over his arm. 'Young Trev's still playing with his plugs and no one else around.'

We spread the rug out over his bath to dry. I looked down at it. 'I wish this bathroom had an outside lock.'

'That doesn't matter. People take rugs on picnics and rugs often get wet.'

'Someone could've seen us from here taking it from the sea.'

'So we've found ourselves some treasure trove. Or have you now fixed fancy man as an inn resident?' I shook my head. 'Angie's out. In any event, the only two windows that overlook where we were are yours and mine. None from the attic looks that way. I've checked.'

I shuddered involuntarily. 'Must be this bathroom that's giving my vibes the creeps. Couldn't we shove that chest across the door again?'

'And advertise to one and all who just happens to have pass keys that we think this is important? When we're still far from sure it is? No. I'll just close the door. You go and have the first bath and then we both need hot strong tea.'

The inn atmosphere was unusual when we went down. It was peaceful and pleasant and had pervaded the lounge to such an extent that even the dead stuffed birds and the flickering shadows seemed cosy. Renny had tea with us. He looked much less tired and quietly elated for a reason he couldn't contain. 'My younger girl has just informed me she expects to make me a grandfather for the first time next April. I must admit I'm rather pleased. She and her husband are delighted as they've been wanting to start a family. But – er – in some respects I find it a somewhat sobering prospect. One might almost say, alarming.'

I thought of Angie's reaction to the prospect of being a step-grandmother and mentally agreed as we congratulated him.

David said, 'I'll bet you'll enjoy it like hell. My dad does. All the fun and none of the hard work, he says.'

I asked, 'Got any snaps of your twins on you?'

Renny chuckled. 'No more than the odd dozen, dear girl, but you two don't want – '

'We do!' We chorused.

David's 'Corr's' and my admiring clucks over his extremely pretty daughters had Renny radiating paternal pride. 'Not bad – not bad – favour their father, naturally. Getting on now. Twenty-six.'

'Same age as Rose.'

Renny shot me a strange reflective glance, then replaced the snaps in his wallet as if they had just sparked off a train of thought he would have preferred not to pursue. I watched David watching Renny over his glasses and didn't notice the door opening until Trevor announced, 'Gentleman to see you, madam!', and ushered in a small, thickset middle-aged man with thinning fair hair, a strong, calm, red face, and the calmest pair of deep-set blue eyes I'd ever seen.

I jumped up smiling. 'Walt! How nice to see you!'

'Thought I'd just come over to see all's well, madam,' said Walt Ames in his slow, broad-vowelled, gentle voice. He nodded to David. 'See you found your way here, Mr Lofthouse.'

David had risen. 'Thanks to you, Mr Ames.'

I introduced Walt to Renny. Walt's head only reached Renny's shoulder but his handshake made the big man wince visibly. 'On your holidays, sir? Good sport?'

'Excellent, thank you, Mr Ames. I'm just taking a lazy afternoon off.'

'And enjoy it the more tomorrow, I shouldn't wonder.'

'Walt, do sit down and have some tea.'

He had on the best suit of working clothes he normally reserved for market days and the county agricultural show. He looked doubtfully at his newly washed boots. 'I don't know as – '

'Nonsense! Everyone wears boots in here. Please.'

'Then I'd not mind a cup. No more. If I can't eat my tea when I get home my wife'll have something to say.'

David went for another cup. He returned before Walt produced the post he had brought for me. 'Young Tom Gillon's on our run again this week so I said to him you'd best leave all hers with me and I'll see she gets it.' He looked at David. 'We don't want no more postcards getting lost do we, sir? You heard about that one, madam?'

'Yes.' I explained it briefly to Renny. 'I expect it may still turn up,' I added.

'I'll be surprised if it does,' said Walt placidly. 'Not if it come when Tom done our run and he's done the last two weeks. Courting he is and I'd not like to say where his mind is, but it's not on his mail. I shouldn't wonder if he handed it in the wrong house. Handed me the two for Mr Denver with mine this morning.' His imperturbable blue gaze rested on my face. 'I heard as he been over here this morning. And taken it hard.'

I nodded. 'I'm afraid so. Understandably.'

'I heard. Nasty do. Mind you, the way that poor young lady drove it'll be small wonder if it were just an accident.

You'd not have caught me driving my sheep down any road when I knew she was due by.'

We had all turned to him, but the men stayed silent. I had to ask, 'Is – is there some question that it wasn't an accident?'

'Not from what I read in my evening paper or saw on the news last night, madam. But seeing there's been more uniforms up Astead Woods today than you could shake a stick at, I'd not like to say.'

Renny leant forward. 'Police searching the woods? Why?'

'They've not said, sir. Least, not as I've heard. All I've heard is the tale this young lad told Sam Parker.' Again, Walt looked straight at me. 'You know Sam Parker, madam. Give him half a chance and he's off.'

'PC Parker, Renny, is our local cop in St Martin's and an eager beaver.'

Walt allowed himself one of his rare smiles. 'PC Barlow, we call him, sir, if not to his face. Knows his job, mind. After he'd a word with this young lad, he'd a word with his duty-sergeant and who he had a word with I'd not like to say but it was after they fetched out the lads with their dogs.'

I glanced at David. He was concentrating on a smoke ring.

'Who's the boy, Walt?'

'Young Billy Adams, madam. You'd not know him. George Adams's lad. Just the one George and his missus got. Astead folk they are and moved to one of the new council bungalows a mile back from Astead crossroads mainland side last year. George works as under-stockman up Astead Hall. Bit slow he is – ninepence in the shilling – but he knows his beasts. Young Billy's ten and a sharp lad they say. Seems he was off school yesterday being just up from flu and the doctor said not back till next week and seeing it was fine he went up to play in the woods. Seems that about a mile up one of the Forestry Commission's tracks in one of their clearings he sees this dark-blue Allegro parked empty.' He nodded to me. 'That's right. Same as Mrs Denver's. And being keen on cars, same as many a lad, he recognizes the make and fetches out his little book to jot the number as he collects car numbers. Then he don't reckon no more to it till he sees the picture of Mrs Denver's car in the evening paper one of the neighbours passes on to his dad, and says he seen it up the woods earlier. Old George being a bit slow didn't reckon nothing to it, but when he gets to work this morning the lads are all talking about the accident so he ups and say what his Billy says. And the head stockman hears.' Walt paused. 'You'll know him, madam. Steve Wattle. Younger brother of Ted, landlord of the Crown in St Martin's. Sharp as they come is young Steve Wattle. He rings up Sam Parker seeing Mrs Denver come from his patch, Sam Parker gets on his motor-bike and runs over for a word with young Billy and the next thing the lads and their dogs are up Astead woods, but for why, I wouldn't like to say.'

I knew Walt. He meant wouldn't, not couldn't.

Renny turned to me. 'You said something the other night about Wattles in St Martin's. I presume they must be related to our friend Harry?'

'I expect so but I'm not sure. Walt, do you know the Harry Wattle from Harbour who works here?'

Walt's smile reappeared. 'I should, madam, seeing his wife's my wife's second cousin. Mind you, their mums not been speaking for years, but we meets weddings, funerals, the like, and old Harry don't let his womenfolk bother him and – no offence, madam – but no more do I. Harry's all right for all he's got a sharp tongue times, and there's not much he don't know about wildfowling as you'll maybe have noticed, sir?'

'Indeed, Mr Ames, indeed. Most interesting,' reflected Renny.

David had decided he was a fly on the wall. A chain-smoking fly with watchful eyes.

Walt drained his cup. 'That went down nicely. Ta. Best be off. If you can spare the minute, madam, you'll like a word about the farm.'

'Yes, of course.'

I left with him and in the corridor asked quietly, 'Anything wrong at the farm?'

'Nah. Nicely. Same as up the house.'

I waited as I knew I must. I had to wait until we were alone in the yard by his estate car. The coachlights were on and the dark air was much colder than last night.

'You didn't mind my fetching Mr Lofthouse over to you, madam?'

I smiled with relief. 'Not at all. I'm glad you did. It's nice seeing him again.'

He didn't smile. 'I heard as he had a bit of bad luck since he come over. Pity about his car.'

I stiffened inwardly. 'Yes. Hear from Harry?' He nodded. 'He tell you about Mr Lofthouse's bathroom?' Another nod. 'And Mr Evans-Williams getting shot?'

'That's right. Real put out over that one is Harry.'

'Poacher, Walt?'

'Seemly, madam. But Harry don't reckon he'll have no more trouble that way and knowing old Harry I don't reckon as he will. Anyone tries it on again and Harry'll shoot first and ask his questions second and he don't miss when he takes aim and there's more than the one as knows it. But that Mr Lofthouse best watch hisself, hadn't he?'

'Why do you say that?'

'Just thinking of my wife,' he replied calmly. 'Got to be a third, she'd say. Always goes in threes. Mind you, I'd say

Mr Lofthouse knows how to watch for hisself. Thirteen pence in the shilling he is, I reckon, and all right for all he's a foreigner. But, if you'll pardon the liberty, madam, same as I said about Tom Gillon – when a young man's courting he don't always keep his mind where he should. You'll not mind my saying that, madam?'

He had used an unnecessary word in that last query. I wished to God I didn't know what it was, or him so well. 'You know how I'll take it, Walt.'

He nodded, but he hadn't finished. He took his tweed cap out of a pocket and smoothed it between his strong, rough hands. 'I was real sorry for you over Mrs Denver. I know as you and she were friendly and you'd be real upset, but you'd best know, madam, there's talk.'

I couldn't and didn't pretend to be surprised. 'About her death?'

'And her carryings on. Don't do to speak unkind of the dead, but you don't need me to tell you what's being said. That young lady been asking for trouble for a long time. Too long many'd say. No offence, madam, seeing she was your friend, but done more than a bit of harm she did, though I'll say this for her – I never reckoned she'd the sense to know harm when she saw it. But when you start up harm, it don't always stop easy, and to my way of thinking,' he added very deliberately, 'some of the harm she started won't stop yet awhile.'

I leant against his car for support. 'Do the police now think she was murdered, Walt?'

'Like I said, they've not said what they think. But police time costs money. They're not having a day up the woods for an accident three miles off on the Ditch road just to give the dogs a run.'

'No. Have – have they heard the talk?'

'If not, they've got cloth ears – and I've never heard as

Sam Parker's hard of hearing. Some say it's a pity Cliffhill's not his patch.'

'Someone from Cliffhill's involved?' I queried carefully.

'No names no pack drill, madam, like we used to say when I was in the army, but I reckon I could put a name to the lad in Sam's mind. Ah well. Best be off.' He slapped on his cap and sniffed the air. 'Don't much like the smell of that sea neither.' He got into his car. ' 'Evening, madam.'

' 'Evening, Walt. Thank you for coming over. Please give my regards to Mrs Walt.'

'I'll tell her.' He touched his cap and drove off looking as solid and unemotional as the sea wall and leaving me as taut as an overstrung violin.

I needed to be alone and to do some hard thinking. I wasn't going to get the chance for either in the yard. One car had already drawn up to wait for Walt's to move off the bridge and the lights of two others were slowing behind it. I went in quickly, intending to collect my post from the lounge and use it as an excuse for retreating upstairs to deal with it. Renny's interest in Walt delayed me. 'David's been telling me he's your farm manager and worked his way up from being the lad who brought out the jugs of cider to the reapers at harvest. Incredible to think only forty years ago the most mechanized agricultural system in the world still reaped by hand. Looks a good, sound man.'

'He is. I'm lucky to have him.'

'Hallo people!' Angie sailed in shedding gloves, a scarlet and black cape and parcels as the leaves in autumn. 'I did some super shopping while Johnnie saw his builder chum and Renny, sweetie, I've brought you the most fabulous cashmere sweater and – ' She was interrupted by an ecstatic, deep-throated East Anglian bellow from the hall.

'Stone me! I won twenty-five quid on old Ernie!'

Two minutes later we were all corral'ed into the celebration party that started in the bar, paused briefly for dinner, and returned to the bar once the coffee we all had in the dining room was finished. It was a good party, even though I had too much on my mind to enjoy it. David seemed to enjoy every moment. He kept insisting on standing rounds, which allowed me to hold back without offending our official hosts, and, as possibly I alone noticed, allowed him to control his own drinks. His control was not apparent.

I had the impression Renny was no more enjoying himself than I was, but was glad of the party for Angie's sake. Renny sat around sipping soda water, smiling and answering pleasantly when addressed, and otherwise relapsing into a preoccupied silence. He was as amused as the rest of us when David, swaying slightly, assumed an Oxbridge accent to suggest, 'I say, chaps, shouldn't we charge our glasses again? Down the hatch, chaps!'

Linda McCabe giggled, 'David, you can mimic nearly as well as Angie!'

Angie leapt off a bar stool to take the floor. 'Oh aye, lad? Happen tha's in t'wrong trade!' she quipped in broad Yorkshire.

David clapped his hands 'Bloody good lass! Do some more!'

Angie was an extrovert in tremendous form and she had had a lot of gin. She mimicked Linda, myself, Mrs Evans-Williams who was behind the bar with Trevor, and then a row of television female personalities and she did it brilliantly. The only problem was that, once started, she was unstoppable. I noticed Nick glancing rather anxiously at Renny and his watch. Linda moved closer to me. 'Can I have some of your chips, Rose?' As I passed them, murmured, 'Nick thinks it's time we broke this up. Renny's awfully tired. Back us?' I nodded. 'Thanks.' She moved back to her husband.

It was after the next outburst of applause that Nick slapped a hand on two of the farmers' shoulders. 'This has been a real great party, guys, but as we all have to be up early I guess this is where we should call it off.'

'Sweetie, no! Don't be such a wet blanket!' Angie flung both arms round Nick's neck and pulled him from the farmers. 'Let your hair down for once, sweetie! Have fun! You can't leave us yet!'

I had caught David's eye and very slight nod. I stood up. 'Angie, I'm terribly sorry, but I'm afraid I'm another wet blanket – '

'You and me both, love.' David staggered over and steadied himself with an arm round my shoulders. 'You be my blanket' – his speech was slurring and smile idiotic – 'and I'll be yours.'

I smiled sweetly. 'Don't kid yourself, chum. Sloshed you may be. In my bed you won't be. I'll get you up to yours but I'm not sleeping with a bottle of whisky.'

'My pal – my pal – ' He kissed my cheek. 'She'll put me to bed – always putting me to bed in another room.'

'That's what friends are for,' I observed to the others.

Even Mrs Evans-Williams joined in the laughter. 'Those two are such old friends,' she remarked to no one in particular, 'grew up together I believe.'

I had still not sorted out which of the farmers had won the twenty-five pounds or their first names as either they were all called Bob or they answered to it. They had drunk the winnings and probably their weight in beer, and at each pint had grown more amiable and amorous. I was glad to have David draped round me for several reasons that included the fact that his breath wasn't inflammable. It took a little longer before we could get away, and it was Renny who finally made it possible.

He rose apologetically. 'It's been grand, chaps, but do

forgive me for backing out now as I'm due for my next jab. If I don't have it you'll be picking me off the floor first.'

'Renny, sweetie, I'd forgotten!' Angie was all concern. 'No, you mustn't be late for your jab. I'll come up with you.'

'No need for that, my dear.'

'Surely not,' put in Nick. 'You stay right here and have yourself a great time, honey. Linda and I will go on up and be right there should Renny require us.'

'You stay along of us!' chorused the farmers. 'You're a great girl, Angie! You stay along of us! Do us another turn – go on – more – more – '

The McCabes and Renny disappeared as they were near the hall door. Angie twirled round on David and me. She hitched back her hair, and smiled at me with her huge eyes glittering with gin, laughter and something akin to triumph. 'Isn't it just too bad that you don't like whisky bottles and have to sleep alone, chum?' she teased in my voice.

David grinned drunkenly and I yelped with laughter. 'How right you are, Angie! I must put this one to bed. Thanks for the party, guys. It's been terrific.'

Johnnie had vanished for most of the evening. He was back in the hall when at last we got out. 'Hope it hasn't been too rowdy for you, Mrs D. They're good chaps. I'll pack 'em off shortly. I won't let them disturb your sleep.' He smiled at David who was now steadying himself on the counter. 'You'll sleep well, old chap.'

David touched his forehead with one forefinger. 'Safe bet, gaffer! Where's me prop?'

'Here, duckie.' I hauled his arm back over my shoulders. 'Just put one foot in front of the other. That's the boy! Now the stairs. Up we go.'

Johnnie called quietly. 'Can you manage him?'

'Yes, thanks,' I called back before David's hand gripped my shoulder. 'I'm used to this of old.'

We were almost at the landing before David murmured, 'I'll sue you for bloody libel.'

'Slander.'

The McCabes and Renny had vanished but as we passed the latter's door he opened it. 'Rose – oh – yes – I'll wait till you get him into his room. Want some help?'

'No, thanks. He's harmless.'

Renny smiled rather curiously and retreated into his room, and closed the door. David gave me a remarkably sober look. 'Your room,' he breathed.

Directly we were in my room he disentangled himself. 'If he asks say I needed your bathroom. If he doesn't, say nowt.'

I stared at him momentarily, then nodded.

Renny came out of his room immediately I opened the fire doors. He looked back at the empty passage before the spoke. 'Rose, I'm sorry to bother you at this late hour, but I rather want a little private chat with you. This seems as good a moment as any. Would you object to my coming along to your room in a couple of minutes after I've had my jab?'

I was very curious. 'Of course not. I'll be up.'

'Thank you.'

I went back to my room. David, looking dead sober, was thoughtfully combing his wet hair as my dressing-table. 'What does he want?'

I told him. 'You must get out. He said private.'

'I'll stay in your bathroom with the light off.'

I sat on the edge of the spare bed. 'Why the big drunk scene?'

'When in Rome.' He came and sat by me. 'Walt tell you anything you didn't know when you got him outside?'

I hesitated, then shook my head. 'Not really. Tell you later. He'll be here any moment.'

'May as well start it now. I'll hear him open his door and shift fast.'

I had time to tell him everything Walt said about Sue and Harry. I hesitated again, then added, 'He thinks you should watch out you don't collect a third.'

'Does he?' He looked at his watch. 'Renny's taking his time.' He suddenly tilted his head to listen. 'You may have to wait longer. Sounds like Angie tripping along.'

'I can hardly hear anything above the voices downstairs.'

'Why worry with Big Ears Lofthouse on hand?'

It wasn't my hearing that worried me. I was thinking about Walt and David's drunk scene. 'Why when in Rome – ?' I began as the first anguished hysterical scream ripped through the walls. It was followed immediately by running footsteps and doors opening and slamming. I would have leapt for my door had David not grabbed me with both hands. 'I'm stoned out of my mind. I've flaked out on this bed and you refuse to add to anyone's problems by shifting me over the road tonight. Understand?' he insisted curtly. 'No arguments!'

'Why the hell – ?' I tried to free myself. 'Something's happened – '

'Of course it bloody has but whatever it is there're enough people to cope with it without you and one's a bloody medic – someone's coming.' He let me go, dropped flat on the bed and rolled over on to his face before we heard the quiet urgent knock.

I had to dry my hand before I could open the door. Linda stood there looking so pale the peeled skin was a rash on her face. 'Nick said I should tell you – ' She broke off at the sight of David. 'He out cold?'

'Yes. Linda, what's happened?'

She put a hand on the lintel to steady herself. 'I shouldn't be so surprised. Nick's been expecting this for months. It's Renny. He's dead.'

I caught my breath. 'Oh, God. How?'

'Heart attack, Nick says. Classic symptoms. He must have just sat down in his chair, given himself his insulin, and gone like that.' She snapped her fingers. 'He looks so peaceful. Asleep. Angie thought he was when she walked in and then' – she shook her head – 'you heard her. Nick and Helen are with her now. He'll give her something as soon as it's safe. She's had so much gin. There's nothing else to be done.' She had another look at David. 'Want him moved? The guys downstairs'll do it.'

I was too shaken for a good lie so I kept to the truth. Some of it. 'No, thanks. You've all got enough to deal with and he'd hate the idea when he surfaces tomorrow. I honestly don't mind and I don't suppose the Evans-Williamses will tonight, though I'd rather you didn't tell them. I owe David a good turn. He's saved my life twice. I'll look after him.'

Her eyes widened, but she was clearly relieved not to have to add to Nick's problems. 'If you're sure – I'll just tell Nick.'

'Thanks. And tell Angie – '

'Not tonight. She's not with us now.'

'I guess not.' I still couldn't take it in. 'Renny dead. Just like that.'

'Nick says that's how it happens with a bad heart attack Too quick even for pain.'

'That's something. He was sweet. I'm so sorry.'

She said flatly, 'He could be sweet sometimes. I'd better get back. I'll tell the others you know and are all right.'

'Thanks. If I can help, give me a shout.'

'There's nothing anyone can do for Renny now, and we'll cope with Angie and – things. Good night.'

'Good night.' I closed and locked the door as David got off the bed.

9

'What the hell are you playing at?' I demanded under my breath.

'Dirty,' he muttered succinctly, thrusting his room key into my hand. 'Beat it to my room, get my airline bag and leave both doors open while you're in there.'

He was neither drunk nor crazy so I did as he said. The passage was empty, all the other doors were shut, and the fire doors muffled the much more subdued rumble of voices coming up from the hall. My hand rattled David's key in the lock and, irrationally, since the passage was empty, I was profoundly thankful David was behind my open door. I turned on the light before I crossed the threshold of his room, grabbed the bag from the bedside table, shot out and relocked the door as if the room were on fire.

He closed my door but didn't lock it. 'Go into my bathroom?'

'God, no. I've seen enough of that rug and the door was closed.'

I could have said the bathroom was on fire from the speed of his reactions. He seized the bag from me, threw it on the bed, pushed me back into the corridor. 'Unlock mine but don't turn on the light. Coast clear?'

I was wrong. He was crazy. And I was a robot. 'Yes.'

The next second he was beside me and pushing me into his darkened room. He closed the door behind us and without turning on the lights groped his way to the bathroom, kicked open the door that was now ajar, before switching on and off the bathroom lights so quickly that I was still blinded when they went out. He said calmly, 'If he was in here he could only have got out of the window and if he did the latch'll be open. You can only open it from inside and I shut it when I nipped up for fags earlier.' We groped to the window. The curtains were closed, the window shut, the latch open, and I hadn't an inch of skin that hadn't risen in goose pimples. 'Yep,' murmured David, moving the curtains a fraction apart. 'Not much of a drop from here. I could use it if I were in a hurry. Far too dark to see anything out this side now. Might have more of a chance if we stuck our heads out for a good look, but that'll advertise the fact that we know he's been in here. If he saw the bathroom light going on and off it was just you charging for that drunken sod's box of tissues as he's started throwing up. Let's get back.' We moved to the door more easily as our eyes had grown accustomed to the darkness. 'All clear?'

'No,' I said without moving my lips.

'Great. You've tucked the sod up in here. Tell whoever's there,' he breathed down the back of my frozen neck.

Nick McCabe had come out of the le Veres' room and seen me. I got through the fire doors first. 'Nick, I'm so desperately sorry about all this.'

'I guess that goes for the most of us, Rose.' His pleasant face was creased with genuine distress. 'Renny was a real nice friendly guy and for his sake I guess we have gotten cause to be grateful his passing was real quick and came about while he was still way up on top of the job and the life he most cared to live. It's kind of hard for Angie to appreciate right now how much he would have resented having to quit shooting, the job, and so on and so forth. Many times of late I have had to warn him that time would be real close if he did not slow down, and so has the specialist in London who has been treating his diabetes these many years. He would not pay heed. Maybe he would take the few hours off like this afternoon, but he was all set to be up early again in the forenoon. He would not stop, so a half-hour back his heart did that job for him.'

'Linda said a heart attack. That mean a coronary?'

'Surely. As classic a one as I have seen, but as I am more a friend of the family than his regular medical attendant, I have already called the local doctor in Harbour and asked him to come right here as I have to have a second opinion. I have no objections to treating the minor injuries of my living friends,' he added gravely, 'but when one passes away I go by the book.'

'Very wise.' I glanced at the le Veres' door. 'Still in there?

'Yes. After the local doc has been we will move his body to the cold store to rest there until such time as the proper arrangements can be made. As of now Angie is with Linda in our room. We have gotten her quietened and are hoping to persuade her to stay with Linda for the night' – he jerked his head at the door – 'and I will sleep right there. We may have ourselves quite a problem as Angie is real set to sleep in there on her own.'

'I can understand that.'

He gave me a blank professional look. 'I guess so. You okay, honey? And David?'

'Yes, thanks.' I gestured towards David's open door and darkened room. 'I've got him to his own bed. He just needs to sleep it off.'

His eyes smiled slightly. 'He's a great guy and he sure knew what he was doing when he picked on you. When do you two plan to get married?'

'We're still arguing over the date.'

'Don't leave it too long.' He sighed. 'Nothing lasts. For good or bad. You kind of think it will, but it does not. Oh, my. I guess I must get back to the girls.'

'Yes, Nick. When you see the Evans-Williamses will you give them my sympathy and say I haven't gone down not to get under their feet.'

'Surely. Goodnight, Rose.'

' 'Night.' I backed through the fire doors and, when he had disappeared into his own room, beckoned David. He vanished while I locked his door and, after I had locked mine, handed me a whisky. 'You rate that. Knock it back.'

'I'll say I do!' I dropped into one armchair. 'Being a tethered goat is bad for my vibes.' I took a drink. 'How did you know someone was sulking in your bathroom and who in hell was it? Fancy man?'

He grinned and sat on the edge of the spare bed. 'Nick's right. I'll have to let you pressure me into wedding you. You're the only woman I've ever met with the nous to act first and ask questions second.'

'Flattery,' I retorted, 'will get you this glass in your face regardless of your glasses. Stop being so bloody evasive. How and who?'

'I just thought I heard someone pussy-footing in there a second or so before I heard Angie's trips and then her blasting off. I wasn't sure I did or who it was, but fancy man's my calculated guess. If it's right – Christ, he sweated when you went in for my bag.'

I said coldly, 'If he was there, him and me, both. Thanks very much.'

'It was only a guess.'

'That latch was open.'

'Yes. That's why I'm personally convinced it was a right guess, but one of the staff could've come in and opened the window to let out the smoke. Every room I use reeks of nicotine. Nevertheless, I'm sure I heard someone creeping in there and, if he was around with Angie's blasts bringing everyone from the bar into the hall and the McCabes into the corridor, he couldn't get out by the main or attic stairs. We were in here so he had to use my room.'

'Which was locked.'

'So what? The helps have pass keys, and the spares are just inside the office door below. Anyone could get hold of one any time, and if he knows his way round this joint, as I'm inclined to think he must,' he went on reflectively, 'then he could be in the habit of using that way out. If so, my moving in there can't have pleased him any and could – just could – account for his wanting Johnnie out.'

I stared at him as my mind ran on the same lines. 'Maybe he fixed your bathroom not to kill anyone just to mess it up and keep the room empty? You said those screws could have been loosened intentionally?'

'And the beams were rotten An idea. I'm not sure I'd bet on it.'

I let it go as I'd had another. 'Think he's one of the staff?'

He shook his head. 'I thought of that. And of the heavy mob. No. The pieces don't fit.' He rang a finger round the rim of his glass. 'Nor does Renny's death.'

'Even though it was – convenient?'

His abstracted eyes looked up slowly. They didn't see me. 'It looks that way and things are often what they look, but even if Renny wanted to tell you something fancy man didn't want you to hear, I can't figure how in hell he knew that. Renny spoke as quietly as we are now. I couldn't hear us from outside that door. If – and God only knows why – fancy man was fool enough to risk hiding out in the le Veres' room – and of all rooms I'd have said that would be the last he'd choose – he couldn't have been anywhere in the bedroom or Renny would've spotted him. The bathroom was his only hope. I don't think he could've heard from there. Nor can I figure why he should kill Renny. Angie's no cop without the backing of her old man's lolly and, as I've said, I'll lay a year's pay she ain't a wealthy widow now.'

I was too shaken by something else he had said to be interested in Angie's attractions. ' "Why he should kill Renny"? So – so – you think like me that, despite what Nick says, it wasn't a coronary?'

'It was a coronary all right! I heard what Nick told you. I believe him. And when they open Renny up at the PM I'm sure Nick'll insist on, I'm sure they'll find he died of a massive great cardiac clot.'

'Then he can't have been killed and if he died at the right moment for someone that was just someone's luck.' He was looking at and seeing me. 'Must be. You can't give someone a coronary to order, can you?' It was a rhetorical question until I saw his expression quicken. 'Can you?' I repeated in another tone.

He blinked at me over his glasses. 'If you know the highly specialized tricks of a highly specialized trade, adrenalin would do the job.' He gave me the details. 'Kills' – he snapped his fingers – 'like so. It produces a condition called arhythmia. Can't ever be proved as it leaves no trace apart from a bloody great coronary.'

'My God, I never knew that.' I lay back in my chair. 'How do you?'

'One of the blokes with whom I got most friendly in Australia was a pathologist who did a lot of forensic work for the cops. He told me.'

'I see.' I blinked. 'No, I don't! That is, I don't see any simple Harbour lad or Angie having that sort of knowledge or knowing how to use it if they did. After all that gin she couldn't have held a syringe steady enough' – I shuddered. 'God. What thought.'

'A thought's all it is and will have to remain as it can never be proved. Be laughed out of court. There was old Renny in his mid-fifties, overweight, flogging himself to keep up with a young wife, at the end of a long day that finished with a knees-up and while he was still dead chuffed about becoming a grandad, sitting down in his chair, giving himself his insulin and out like a light. Classic, as Nick and the entire medical profession would agree. The poor bloke was a bloody sitting duck for his fatal coronary.'

I remembered his using that description in another context two evenings ago and, from the way he gulped some whisky, so did he. We didn't refer to it. I said absently, 'Of course, if you could've picked up that trick at second hand, possibly – ' Then I remembered what we had both forgotten and leapt up. 'David! The rug!'

'Cool off, it's safe.' He stood up, and heaved back the mattress of the spare bed to expose the mohair rug neatly folded in two between the mattress and the canvas cover over the bedsprings. 'I shifted it in here when I nipped up for those fags while you were outside with Walt. I still had your key as I'd forgotten to give it back before tea. The rug had stopped dripping. That's an obvious hiding place but, as there's often the chance that the obvious gets overlooked, I used it. And take that dirty look off your face! I'd no idea then that fancy man would turn up – if he did. If he did, I'm damned glad I brought it in here though I still stick by my original theory that neither he nor anyone else would have come looking for it as no one knows we got hold of it. Right bonus for him had he seen it in my bathroom.'

I recovered my breath. 'If so sure, why bring it in here?'

'You. You've changed much more than I thought. In the past what you call your instincts and I prefer to call your judgement was so lousy that every time you made a forecast I knew I'd only to reverse it to get close to the right answer. Not now. You've either acquired, or allowed to come to the surface, the handy if disturbing knack of being right far more often than wrong. I decided to back you on this one, and if fancy man was here I sure put my money on the right horse.'

I could have done without the compliment. It reminded me too disturbingly of my reaction to Walt's visit. 'The fundamental reason for the big drunk scene?'

'You could say that. A greater love hath no man than he who risks lumbago – '

'I thought paddling was the ultimate sacrifice?'

He smiled quickly. 'Neck and neck. Sit down, love.' He pushed me gently back into the chair, sat on the arm and rested one of his along the back. 'Tell me properly what Walt said to you outside.'

I told him in detail and that took time. During that time we heard a car drive up, and not long after, driving away; and then the sound of the men carrying Renny's body down to the cold store. Slowly the footsteps, many more footsteps, came quietly back up, and doors were closed carefully and the lights went out below, and appeared in the flat opposite, but no voices reached us. The silence of death shrouded the inn more tangibly than the darkness of the night. It did not silence us as we weren't there, we were in Astead woods, but it made us lower our already low voices.

David said, 'That kid must've seen more than the empty parked car.'

'I think so too, though Walt didn't say more. But he didn't even spell out the blunt instrument they must be looking for.' Our eyes met. 'You must be right about her having the wrong head injury. Can't have been the tree.'

'Probably a heavy spanner. That would do it, but they won't find it if they search the woods till doomsday. It'll be down at the bottom of a dyke and it won't float off through the outlet and come back with the tide ' His gaze had moved to the spare bed. 'They can't dredge every dyke on the marsh.'

'No.' I looked at the bed. 'That rug must've got out just as the tide was on the turn – ' I broke off. 'I mustn't let that confuse me. It's nothing to do with Sue. Or' – I smiled without humour – 'are you going to suggest Gordon's fancy man?' I answered myself. 'Of course, he can't be. He was fighting it out with Sue at Midstreet, while Angie was keeping a date with hers outside here our first evening. But if Sam Parker's already on to Gordon, I can't follow why the cops haven't checked that phone call with me.'

'They will. Like the mills of God they may grind slow but they grind exceeding small.'

'I suppose so. Hell.' I rested my head against him and closed my eyes. 'Probably tomorrow. And probably tomorrow I'll have to have with Angie a variation of the heart-to-heart with Francis this morning – God! Was it only this morning?' I looked up at him. 'I am a nutter, David. I can't stop wondering – who'll I have it with the day after tomorrow.'

'You're no nutter. Just whacked and getting carried away again, love.' He kissed me gently. 'Let it go for the night. Not that there's much of it left.'

I looked at his watch. 'Nor there is. Going back to your room?'

'No. You don't like my pyjamas and I'm not unpacking another pair tonight. Do you want the bathroom first or can I have it?'

'You have it first,' was all I said. He disappeared into the bathroom and for the first time since Walt drove off I felt safe.

I felt safe for a full five minutes, as that was the length of time he took in the bathroom. He had just turned off the taps when Angie simultaneously called and knocked softly, 'Rose, as your light's on – still up? Can I come in? Please? Just for a few minutes?'

David silently opened the bathroom door, put a finger to his lips, mouthed something and beckoned.

'Just coming, Angie.' I moved quietly to David. 'What?'

He gripped my shoulders and looked into my eyes urgently. 'Don't leave this room for any reason or say I'm here,' he breathed. 'Understand?'

Only the English language. I had turned back into Robot Rose. I nodded, he turned off the bathroom lights and backed behind the half-closed door.

I went over mechanically and unlocked my door. 'Come in, Angie – and I'm so sorry.'

'Bless you, sweetie.' She laid her cold cheek against mine and kissed the air.

She wore a long black velvet kaftan with silver embroidery round the neck, hem, sleeves and marking the long slits of the deep pockets. She had removed most of her make-up and looked older, and very sad. Either the shock and distress, or whatever Nick had given her, seemed to have sobered her completely. She walked over and sat in one armchair with such studied solemnity that I had the uncharitable impression she was making a stage entrance. She adjusted the skirts of her kaftan with dignity, then folded her hands in her lap and gracefully lowered her dark head. 'I feel awful intruding on you like this, sweetie, but I couldn't sleep and saw your lights still on and' – slowly her great, dark, red-rimmed eyes looked round the room – 'I thought you'd probably be alone and hoped you wouldn't mind. Boy friend snoring his head off?'

I sat in the other armchair. 'He wasn't snoring when I last saw him. Just quiet.'

She forced a smile. 'Fabulous party man, isn't he?'

'When he gets going.'

'Such a sweetie. Renny liked him. I could tell. I expect you could, with your husband?'

'I expect most wives can.'

She lowered her eyes. 'And widows – remember. It's all right, sweetie, you don't have to answer that. I've just found it out for myself.' She paused and breathed as if she had been running. 'Oh, I know – I know he wasn't always a perfect sweetie but for God's sake who expects perfection and wouldn't one be bloody bored if one got it? But Renny was so – so – ' She looked up with eyes filled with tears that could have been genuine. I didn't think they were, but I realized I could be wrong. 'Renny was just so human and so sensible and – well – he was always there and so – so – wonderfully reliable. Of course, he was years older than me, but that never mattered and anyway if you've had any experience of men – you have and I have – my God, young men are so demanding! So selfish! All they care about is themselves! You take my advice, sweetie – find yourself an older man. Much better be an old man's darling than a young man's slave – I remember my first! He was such a sod! I just couldn't believe my luck when I married Renny – and now' – she sighed tragically – 'now I can't believe it's all over.'

I didn't say much as she needed a listener, just as Francis this morning. Only with her I found listening more exhausting than painful. The more she talked, the sadder I grew for Renny.

She talked and talked: of their marriage; of Renny's first marriage; of his twins; his friendship with Johnnie. On and on. 'Poor old Johnnie is absolutely knocked out by this. Renny was his best and oldest friend. Everyone's knocked out. We were having such a fabulous party – we've always had a fabulous time at Harbour and those two did so love fighting their war again. God, sweetie, I feel such a bitch now – the times I've said, yawn – yawn – not back to that damned desert. And now' – she smiled a sad little smile – 'do you know what I've just been doing?'

I shook my head. I was so tired, I was having a full-time job trying to keep awake. 'Tell me.'

'I've – most people would think me crazy but you won't – I've actually been sitting looking at his tatty old war souvenirs. His toys he called them. Men are such little boys. He took them with him everywhere. I knew you wouldn't mind my showing you and I had to show someone.' She drew from one of her pockets an old tarnished cap badge. 'Tank Corps. He wore that at Alamein.' She put it away and produced a small bit of dark twisted metal. 'Shrapnel. He always said this should have killed him in forty-three. Imagine?' I nodded. 'It got stuck in the silver cigarette case he always kept in the left-hand breast pocket of his battledress jacket.' She put away the shrapnel. 'This was his most beloved toy.' She took a much larger and darker metal object from her capacious pocket and suddenly I was wide awake. She stroked the revolver lovingly. 'It's a Lüger. Did you know?'

'No. I've heard of them. I wouldn't recognize one.'

She sighed, lost in memories. 'Renny said he took it off a dead German officer. He wouldn't go anywhere without it. Even brought it along on our honeymoon. He called it his lucky mascot. Poor sweetie.' She pointed the gun at me and smiled gently. 'It's all right, Rose. Renny never kept any guns loaded. I'll show you.' She turned the gun towards the beds, cocked it, released the safety catch and pulled the trigger. It clicked harmlessly. 'See?' Her smile widened as she swung the gun back at me. And suddenly her smile terrified me. 'Quite safe.' Again she pulled the trigger harmlessly. 'What did I say? I'll just put the safety catch back on.' She dropped her left hand over the gun without altering its direction and seemed to pull back the working parts. There was another, rather different and much fainter click. I assumed it was made by the safety catch falling back into place and was about to breathe out mentally and physically. I didn't remember doing either.

David had streaked from the bathroom and pulled the Lüger out of her hands before we knew he was there. He held the gun out in front of her and broke it open. 'You want to be careful with these things, Angie,' he said very deliberately. 'You obviously didn't know this but, as you can now see, there are a couple of magazines left in this butt. If you had just pulled this trigger for fun again, as the gun was aimed straight at Rose, from where you are sitting you would have shot her through the heart. I know that would have upset you very much – and it would have upset me very much.'

She had clasped her face and was gazing at him in horror. She did the only intelligent thing. She went straight into acute hysterics. 'Leave her, Rose, and get Nick.' David pushed the Lüger into one of his pockets. 'Tell him why. Exactly.'

I didn't hesitate though my legs felt weaker than on my first day up after flu. Nor did Nick after my terse explanation. He seized a dressing-gown and his medical bag but didn't bother with slippers. 'I guess she's too overwrought and what with all she's had tonight she just does not know what she is doing,' he said over and over.

In an icy, authoritative voice I had never heard David use before, he cut Nick short. 'Take her back with you, Nick, and don't leave her alone again tonight. If she's not responsible for her actions, then you are. Deal with her.' He ushered them out, closed and locked my door, pulled me into his arms and held me very tightly. Neither of us said anything until I stopped shaking. 'David. I – I honestly think she wanted to kill me.'

'I know she did.'

I jerked back my face from his to look at him. 'Why?'

'I don't know for sure. I'll tell you this, Rose. By Christ, I'm bloody finding out and bloody fast.'

I had seen him look angry before but never as angry as this. He looked ready to murder.

'You can't do more tonight.' I kissed his mouth. 'Come to bed, David.'

IO

I hadn't been asleep long when I woke suddenly. I could think of more than a few reasons for that, but I couldn't hear one. Not at first. David was a quiet sleeper, there was no wind, not even a breeze, the inn was as silent as the tomb it had become for Renny, and the sea was lazily roaring as it dragged out the pebbles. I must've slept longer than I thought for the tide to be going out. It had been high water when we were in the nethouse.

I freed an arm, flicked on David's lighter, looked at both our watches on my bedside table and knew what had woken me. Only ten to three. The tide wasn't going out, it was coming in. It wouldn't be high for about fifty minutes. Life might be full of little surprises, like a woman I'd never set eyes upon until three evenings ago attempting to murder me tonight; Francis getting his sums right about Sue – and myself; fancy man's apparent fixation with David's room and – if only in my mind – determination to destroy all · traces of that rug for a reason I still couldn't fathom; or my now gladly sharing a bed with a man I had thought out of my life and 12,000 miles away when I arrived at Harbour. but there were no surprises about the times of the tides. If the sea now sounded as if it were going out there was something wrong with either my hearing or the sea. I raised my head, and listened intently. It was the sea. Something about it sounded as wrong as something Sue had said in that telephone call.

What had she said? And it was then that, with the crystal

clarity that can come to the mind in the small hours, I realized what had been worrying me was not anything she said, but the way she sounded. My subconscious had given me the pointer when I told David I'd never heard her in such a state. That was it. Literally, I'd never heard Sue's drawl sound so affected, her whine so petulant – in fact, all her vocal mannerisms so accentuated – as accentuated as mine when my voice had come out of Angie's mouth at the party. . . . My God! I must be crazy! Of course it had been Sue. Francis had said that Sue said at breakfast she was going to ring me – Sue always had rung when she wanted to bleat – and she'd rung from Astead crossroads when Angie had been with the shooting party three miles south of Lymchurch. Lymchurch itself was twelve cross-marsh miles from Astead crossroads – and I was stark raving mad!

David wasn't mad and he thought Angie had wanted to kill me.

My shivers penetrated his sleep. 'What's up, love?' he muttered tenderly. 'Nightmare or just cold?'

'Just thinking. The sea woke me. It sounds odd. Listen.'

He lifted his head. 'Sounds just like the sea to me. Wonderful thing, nature, but not so wonderful as you. How do you manage to be so gloriously devoid of bones? Mmmmm?'

'Just a minute.' I held back his face. 'Sorry I woke you but as you are awake I'd like to take a look from the marsh window. Just for a minute. I won't put on the light. I've been awake long enough to see my way without.' I disentangled myself, got out of bed, dived about for my kaftan and found it on the floor. I pulled it on. 'I must see what the sea's doing as it sounds wrong.'

He groaned, raised himself higher and flicked on the lighter to see the time. 'Lofthouse, you're a failure. Not just slipping,' he announced sadly, 'but bloody washed-up. Took you nearly three years to get her into bed and inside of an hour she's up and off. Prefers looking at the sea. Nothing for you but booze and nicotine. Mind if I smoke in bed, Rose?'

'Not if you don't set the bed alight.'

'What matter if I do?'

'Stop griping. I'm only being a good citizen.'

'Huh! "Can't do more tonight," you said. "Come to bed," you said. You didn't say anything about getting up to bung your thumb in the sea wall. Warn me before you open the window – nasty dangerous stuff, fresh air. And don't fall out. I don't fancy having to explain to the coroner why I bedded you with a loaded Lüger under me pillow.'

'I didn't know you'd put it there.'

'A failure,' he mused, lighting up, 'but perhaps not a total failure.'

I turned at the window to smile at him in the darkness. 'We'll have to agree to differ on both counts. You kipper your lungs a few more moments. I can see pretty well through the glass as the curtains are open' – I faced the window – 'and thank God you do. I can't bear sleeping with them shut.'

'You mean you actually sleep at night?'

'Belt up! We sea-watchers need to concentrate.'

'Bet you can't even see it in this dark.'

'I can.'

That was true. Dawn was still hours off, but the night outside was lighter than earlier as the clouds were higher, thinner, and had just sufficient movement to let through occasional slivers of light from the weak youngish moon and the isolated patches of stars. The marsh was a black quilt ruched with the faintly lighter shadows of the dyke rushes, edged by the low, solid, darker curving shadow of the wall, and the flat unbroken black sea beyond. A sluggish, waveless sea that had a very heavy smell from the way it was still dragging down the pebbles. 'Fresh air coming.'

'Sadist.' He stubbed out his cigarette and covered his head, so he didn't see my hand suddenly freeze on the unreleased latch. I pressed my face against the glass and lost interest in the sea. I was no longer at all sure it was what had woken me, but I wanted to be sure before I said anything. That took a few moments as the shadows up against the inn were so dark. Then the the particular shadow that had caught my attention a few yards down on my right moved again. None of the other shadows were moving because the air was so still, and none looked like anything but shadows. The one I was watching had a just discernible form. Then it moved again and I was sure. It was a man and either a stout man or one in a very bulky jacket, with a cap on his head but no boots on his feet. He was moving too lightly.

'David, I think he's back,' I whispered urgently. 'Put on your glasses and come quick.'

'All I bloody needed,' he muttered, but joined me. 'Where?'

'Right below us and moving towards that corner of the yard. I picked him up under your window. See? That sort of slow ripple in the shadows against this wall?'

He peered and shook his head. 'No. My night vision's lousy. Sure?'

'Positive. He's going round into the yard.'

I slid over to a yard window. He hitched up his enveloping eiderdown and I thought had followed. Instead he was getting dressed at the double. 'Going after him?'

'Or has he vanished?'

The coachlights were out and the buildings on either side cast deeper shadows over the flags and those against the walls were black. Again it was the movement that was the giveaway. 'No. He's moving up against this wall towards the kitchen end.' David was pulling on another sweater. 'I'd like to believe he's an honest-to-God burglar. I can't. Must be fancy man. Why? Rug?'

'Not knowing can't say. Think I should ask him?'

'I think you should go down, wake Harry, and ring the cops.'

'They'd be dead chuffed to be hauled out miles at this hour for a bloke merely lingering with or without intent who'll have vanished before they get here. Where's he now?'

'Still by the kitchen – no – he's going over –' David was beside me before the shadowy figure streaking lightly over the yard disappeared into the blackness against the garage doors. 'Maybe he's just a car thief – yes – he's moving along the garages. He must be after Renny's Rolls – no – moved on – blimey!' I seized his arm. 'My garage.'

He said mildly, 'Yep. Must fancy Allegros. I must ask him that – let go, love –'

'No! Wait. He's going to break in –' I broke off as the figure opposite stepped a little back and for once was out of the shadows. I saw clearly his back and his hand moving into a pocket. He seemed to drop something small. I didn't see it fall or hear any clink, but it apparently sounded like a thunderclap to him. His head jerked over his shoulder and his face jerked up to look at the upper windows of the inn just as a sliver of moonlight broke through. The next moment it had gone, the man was flattened in the shadows, and I felt as if I'd been flattened by a bulldozer. 'David! Did – did – you?'

'Yep. Even with my eyes. Figures.'

He made for the door.

I shook my head incredulously. 'It doesn't. It's – plain crazy –'

'Nothing crazy about this. Smart operator. In, yet?'

'I just don't – yes – going in – but you mustn't –'

'Waste more time. Stick there. When you see me below, if he's still inside, open and shut a window. If he's moved off, do nowt. Stay put, lock this door and guard that rug. If you're right,' he added tersely, 'Gordon could need it.' He was gone.

I didn't waste any more time. I watched my garage door as I backed for a sweater, slacks and socks. I was dressed when David's sturdy outline emerged from the side door beyond the telephone alcove. I opened and closed a window silently. He raised one arm in acknowledgement. I didn't wait to watch him cross the yard. I hadn't to wait long for him to appear; just long enough for everything that had happened since I came to Harbour to flick through my mind like a speeded-up film. That most of the frames still made no sense was, I suspected, as I either had them in the wrong order or was looking at them from the wrong angle. What made frightening sense was the thought that a murderer who had killed twice wouldn't be too fussy over the third.

I hauled out the near-dry rug, rolled it, stuck it under one arm and the Lüger in my slacks pocket. The gun was hideously uncomfortable but I preferred that to the thought of leaving it behind. I had a final quick check out of the window. David had disappeared.

The silence was throttling when I tore down the passage and stairs. I heard Harry's snores before I opened the unlocked office door. I went in and closed it before I switched on the light and he sat up with a snort, blinking angrily.

'Harry, we've just seen a man breaking into my garage. David's gone over, I'm following.' I dumped the rug on his bed. 'Keep this safe – give it only to the police or me – and if anything goes wrong tell the police and Walt Ames we both recognized the man. His name's Francis Denver.'

In answer he grunted and glared at me. Walt said he was all right which meant Walt trusted him. I trusted Walt.

I hoped to God we were both right and turned off the light before I let myself out. I heard his curses as he stumbled for the switch, and paused on one foot to peer through a hall window but saw nothing but the empty yard. I raced on down the residents' corridor and out through the closed, unlocked side door.

I had let myself out very quietly from instinct, not intention. I had intended charging straight over to my garage, but instinct and the silence kept me pressed against the door for several moments. The silence was unnerving; it made the sea sound uncannily close and made me for once grateful for the homely croaks of a handful of insomniac frogs. I could see my garage door was just ajar, but I couldn't hear one sound coming from inside. Then a figure that wasn't David's glided from the door and swiftly made for the bridge end of the building and disappeared round the corner. He had gone so fast against the wall that I couldn't have stopped him even had I been an expert shot with the Lüger and there been no law to restrain me. I wondered why he had gone that way and not back to the inn but was far too concerned for David to dwell on any other matter. I ran over to the garage and heard his blasphemous mutters before I pulled open the door and switched on the light. He sounded hurt.

He was hurt. He was trying to haul himself from the floor by the locked handle of the driver's door. There was blood streaming down the side of his face from a gash over his left eyebrow and his hair and shoulders glinted with glass splinters. The remains of his glasses were on the floor at his feet. 'Oh, my poor darling – ' I rushed to him.

'Poor bloody moron – let him see me first – ' he mumbled in a daze and went on fighting the locked handle. 'Got to get this out – my car – ' He swayed violently and crumpled on to the floor.

I opened my mouth to yell for Harry, then closed it with a snap. I had realized what David meant. Fewer people around till the car was clear the better. One set of my car keys were in my room but I kept the spare set in the bottom of the box of tissues in the dashboard shelf. Car thieves were less of a problem on the marsh than the miles between one's home and the nearest garage, and repairing a window cost less than a lock. I looked around quickly, found an old rag lying in one corner of the floor, wound it round my hand and wrist, turned my back to protect David and myself, and broke the driver's window with the butt of the Lüger so easily that had I not been so frightened and angry I'd have been very pleased with myself. A couple of seconds later I backed out as if from a pit at Brands Hatch. I saw David raising himself on an elbow and that the floor beneath the car was clear. As David said, a smart operator – who must now be convinced luck loved him, and David's unexpected appearance had proved the cherry on top. . . . Rose, my dear treasured friend, you don't know how I hate to say this, but wasn't I right? His own was the dress rehearsal – you'll remember he wasn't hurt at all. He crept down in the night to set up yours to get you. Not the first man to try to kill the girl he loved rather than let anyone else get her . . . thank God he slipped up. . . .

I swung the car back hard left to drive out forward and passed the hall door as Harry charged out slapping on a cap and zipping up a shooting-jacket. He shouted something I couldn't catch. I didn't know if he'd recognized me in the darkened interior, or thought I was stealing my car. I daren't risk any time on explanations until I had the car up on the marsh road well clear of the buildings. I had to slow on the cinder road before crossing the bridge and taking the sharp turn that was necessary either left or right. I wasn't absolutely certain my car was a danger; I was one hundred per cent certain of the dangers of the lining dykes.

I made a calculated guess before I was off the bridge. If the car was safe it wouldn't matter which way I turned. If Francis had fixed up something with a long enough fuse to let him get clear – and he was a mining engineer – I guessed his main object must be to create a diversion that would, forseeably, empty the inn. The nearest fire station was eighteen miles away. Unless every available pair of amateur hands got on the job at once, the garages and flat, being half-timbered, could be a bonfire before the professional firemen arrived. That would leave Francis free to nip quietly back into the inn for whatever it was he wanted to find or do. And if I was right over all this, then the obvious place for him to hide and wait was on the stretch of sea road hidden from the inn windows by the opposite building. No one would hang around the flat windows that side with a garage below on fire, and on that bit of road he'd have a nice wide dyke between him and the blaze.

Directly I swung the car towards the sea, the headlights picked up his crouching figure, huddled between dyke rushes and the road edge on the far left. He didn't look up at the car. He seemed to be studying something in one hand. The thought flashed into my mind; the bastard's doing a count-down on a stop-watch. That was my last coherent thought for quite a long time.

I stood on the brake and clutch. The car slithered to a stop about ten yards from where I had first seen him. He hadn't waited. Once he realized I was stopping by him, he reacted like an Olympic sprinter to the starter's pistol and raced down the road as if his gold were at stake. There was no need to guess why. I switched off the engine, but left on the headlights and leapt out. I ran faster than I knew I could and was over the bridge when my car exploded. I heard later that, unlike David's, there had been no visible smoke from the bonnet and the first sheet of flame seemed to come from the boot.

Suddenly I was surrounded by heavily breathing men wearing shooting-jackets and boots over pyjamas, demanding in East Anglian, Canadian and marsh voices what the hell was going on. The only man I properly noticed wore an old duffle coat over a dressing-gown and a sling hanging round his neck and wasn't asking anything. Johnny Evans-Williams stood at the edge of the cinder track staring not at the blaze across the dyke but down towards the sea. In the light of the other men's torches the expression on Johnnie's face was the expression of a man looking straight into hell. Then David's powerful shoulders blocked out the others as he pushed his way through, half-blind without his glasses. He steadied himself with one hand on my shoulder and mopped the blood from his left eye with the other. 'I was not kidding, love, when I said you're making an old man of me. You all right?'

I nodded breathlessly. 'But the bastard's got away – '

'Only *pro tem*. All the blokes saw him running in your heads and – ' He never finished the sentence. The sound that silenced him deafened us all. It was the sound of an explosion further off down the marsh that, in comparison, reduced the sound of my car exploding to the popping of a paper bag.

Harry recognized it first. 'Wall's give! Sea's coming! In and up all! In and up all!'

Other men shouted and somewhere a woman screamed. I thought I just heard Johnnie's agonized 'The boy – ' before all human voices were drowned by the gigantic roaring of the sea battering through the wall, tearing away concrete blocks as if they were pebbles, and hurtling back into the stranded harbour with the terrifying, unmeasurable elemental power of millions of tons of suddenly unleashed water.

Though the inn was on the natural mound of one old arm

and we had only yards to run to the hall door, before we reached it the sea had spilled over the arms and was surging and boiling ankle-deep over the flags. It was nearly over the eighteen-inch flood-sill of the hall door, when Harry slammed and bolted it, and slammed down the flood-board fixed to the inside. The farmers, being fenmen, had already organized themselves into anti-flood squad with the speed born of experience, and disappeared to ensure every ground-floor window and door was securely locked, every flood-board down, and every available cushion and movable chair seat piled against the bottoms of the windows.

'I guess I best take a look at your face, Dave – '

'You take him up for that, doctor,' barked Harry. 'I'll not say she'll come in below and I'll not say she'll not. Inn'll hold. Done it afore. Get on up all as isn't wanted down here to watch.' He rounded on Trevor who had now appeared white-faced in a hastily pulled on T-shirt and jeans. 'Fetch out candles smart, lad. Lights'll go soon as she gets the pylons and she'll get ours. Mayn't be wetting many feet in Harbour but she'll fetch out the electricity.' He looked at Johnnie who was now sitting on a stool in the empty bar with his arms propped on the counter and his head in his hands. He seemed oblivious to the roaring that was still going on outside, and what was happening inside and to his inn. His wife, in a fur coat over nightclothes, stood by him with one arm round his sagging shoulders. I hadn't noticed her in the yard or known she was up, until I saw her watching Johnnie with a strange mixture of distress and relief on her thin, pinched, greyish face. 'Best to get the guv'nor upstairs, madam,' said Harry in a gentler tone. 'Best get him up.'

'Yes, Harry. Thank you.' She leant closer to Johnnie and whispered something. He didn't seem to hear.

Nick had gone up ahead. I said quietly, 'Can you manage the stairs alone, David? I think Johnnie needs more help.'

'Yep. He will.' He removed his arm from my shoulders and brushed his mouth against my ear to add, 'His son, I'll bet.'

I stared at his blood-caked face and painfully bloodshot eyes. 'What – ?' But as I mouthed the demand I remembered how Johnnie's smile had reminded me of something I couldn't place and how my caricature of Francis had so unaccountably – then – turned into one of Johnnie. And I remembered that first terrible triumphant roar of the returning sea and Johnnie's cry of anguish. I nodded and went into the bar. 'Can I help you get your husband upstairs, Mrs Evans-Williams?'

She said calmly, gratefully. 'Thank you, my dear. He's so shocked – Renny's death – you understand?'

'Yes,' I said, and our eyes met, but whether she knew how much or how little I understood, I couldn't tell.

We took him along to my room as Nick, with Linda's help, was dealing with David's face in there. We had Johnnie on the spare bed when all the lights failed. Linda drew me aside. 'Thank God Angie's still flat out. I've just had another look at her. Hasn't stirred since Nick sent me back after we heard your car – ' She had to break off as Nick needed her to hold one of the candles Trevor had brought in earlier.

'You'll be just fine after a good rest, Johnnie. You have had a real traumatic time – just take it real easy.' Nick turned back to David and took another thorough look by torchlight in both eyes. 'No glass. I guess you were in real luck. None has gotten in that I can trace.'

'That was his one slip-up.' David spoke very softly. 'He blinded me with the torchlight before he used the other end on my glasses. Then finished the job with a neat chop on the back of the neck. But for that light, he might've done the job for good.'

'Land sakes, Dave, why would the guy want – ' Nick's voice stopped abruptly. There wasn't enough light for me to see how David had silenced him, but I saw Johnnie raise his head momentarily then flop back and close his eyes.

'Thanks, Nick.' David got out of the armchair. 'I'll get my spare glasses.'

'I'll get them. In one of your suitcases?'

'Small one, love. Two pairs. Either'll do.'

I took one of the candles with me, stood the pewter holder on the chest in David's room, found his glasses, and before returning with them took the candle into the bathroom. I was examining the few traces of sand and mohair at the bottom of the bath when David joined me. I handed him his glasses, he put them on and bent over the bath. 'Can't have done his blood-pressure much good when he switched on his torch in here. He's bound to have done that not to knock into anything. And then he had to come back.'

'And create a diversion to clear this joint.'

'Sure did.'

Without saying more we moved to his room window and leant out. The sea had quietened. It had regained its lost entry and was satisfied to lick round the inn and ripple gently over the drowned marsh, dykes and road. It was not much more than a couple of feet deep round the inn, but the marsh we were overlooking was fifteen feet below sea-level and twenty feet below the inn. From the inn to the sea wall there was nothing to see but the water growing blacker as the sky was imperceptibly growing lighter, and the gap that looked to have been bitten out of the wall by giant teeth.

David said, 'I thought you said the Endels had finished off all the dragons.'

'We must've slipped up.'

'Even Homer sometimes nods,' he allowed wearily, 'and

you weren't around then. You didn't slip over that rug. Still under Johnnie?'

'No. Harry – oh God – better check.'

We found Harry dealing with the flooded telephone alcove. 'Nah. Not come from outside. Come up from the cellars. She got in the lot and the cold store. Not done the birds no good I shouldn't wonder but Mr le Vere, he'll not be bothered. Rug? It's safe. That's what you said, wasn't it? Bunged it in the guv'nor safe. Waterproof it is, I got the keys.' He thumped his middle. 'On me belt. Wanting it now?'

David and I looked at each other in the candlelight. He said, 'If it's not too much of a bother now, Harry?'

'Nah. She's going down. Be out soon. Soon dry off. Up here, mind. Harbour'll stay a harbour till they mends the wall and that'll take a day or two I shouldn't wonder.' He put down his bucket and squelched ahead of us to the office. He didn't ask why we wanted the rug or another question about it. No one else asked any more questions during what remained of that night. Consequently, it was not until the morning that Nick McCabe discovered why Angie had slept so soundly through it all and Linda was unable to wake her.

'Brisbane.' David took another sip of the Chief Constable's whisky. 'Only time I was there was the day I flew out and wrote and posted that card to Rose while waiting for my flight. Yet that morning by the nethouse when, as we did, he must've spotted the faint fuzz on the fodder, he seemed to know I'd been there. Could have been just coincidence – just the first place in Australia that came into his head – but as the other coincidences we've described seemed to be piling up, I started wondering if he had some reason for wanting Rose out of Endel and at Harbour.'

The Chief Constable took another look at the two-day-old strapping over David's left eyebrow and reached for his tobacco jar. 'Understandably.'

We were alone with him in his study. Yesterday, we had spent a couple of hours alone with two senior CID men in Astead's main police station, and last evening an hour alone with Mrs Evans-Williams in her flat. The Chief Constable had just told us that, around the time we were in the flat, an Astead police car had driven Gordon back to his lodgings in Cliffhill. The CID men yesterday had told us Gordon's full name was Gordon Alan Robertson and that since the previous evening he had been helping with their enquiries. Shortly after we left them, the coastguards had found Francis's body trapped between displaced concrete blocks, and an hour or so later they had fished out the Audi that had been flattened like a stamped-on sardine tin.

'Car's in a shocking mess,' said the Chief Constable, 'but

the forensic chaps have managed to find what they expected in the boot. Yes. He had her body there wrapped in the rug. Those stains were made by her blood and I'm informed she was wrapped in it immediately after death. The chaps are very pleased with themselves and you for that rug. It was precisely what they told us to look for after they found the few strands of mohair in the hair, on the clothes, and then in the boot of the Allegro. Could've given us no small problem had he used a plastic groundsheet, but obviously he decided wool would be warmer. Had to keep the body warm as long as possible. New rug, my chaps say. We know he didn't buy it locally, and as you've said you've never seen it in his car, Rose, presumably he brought it elsewhere and kept it in the boot for this purpose.'

'Christ,' muttered David, and I grimaced.

'Yes. Unpleasant thought.' He filled his pipe, carefully. 'That fatal blow worried the police surgeon too. He drove out to look at the ash and decided the damage couldn't have been made by a human skull without its being smashed like an eggshell. He thought it had been caused by some heavy implement wrapped in something similar to her leather hat held in the hand of an outstretched arm swung right back before swinging forward and hitting the tree with great force. Most probably a man, he said, though a strong woman could've done it. Suggested we started looking for an implement and the rug. We didn't expect to find either in the woods as we were pretty sure both were in dykes, but had to look.' He lit his pipe with one match. 'You're right. She was killed nearly two hours earlier than was first assumed. We now put the time somewhere between ten a.m., when we know she left the hairdresser, and ten-thirty a.m., when young Billy Adams spotted her apparently empty car in the clearing. The boy's quite definite about the time. He's just had a new watch for his birthday a few days back and consults it every couple of minutes. We think Denver had already killed her and put her body in the boot when he heard the child, and hid in the trees until Billy wandered back down the track. It's a mile down that track to the main road. Billy says he had only gone a short way when the Allegro went slowly by driven by "a lady wearing a floppy browny hat, browny coat and dark glasses" and disappeared round the next bend. That track's all bends. Denver, of course.'

I said mechanically, 'Sue was always borrowing his shirts and sweaters as they were the same height and build. And she always kept dark glasses in her dashboard shelf. With the hat pulled down and glasses, with his pale skin he could easily have looked like a woman from a few yards off.'

David said, 'The kid must've seemed a bonus. Further proof that Sue was still alive, and to cover his alibi she had to seem that until around noon. I imagine once well down the track he took a side path to where he'd hidden his Audi. Have any tyre tracks been found?'

The Chief Constable nodded. 'The ground's always damp and thick with old leaves in those woods and, as the trees are still so heavy with leaves, one could conceal a tank a few feet from the paths with very little effort. He'd chosen a nice snug corner. Quite nice sets of tyre marks, I'm informed, but, of course, he wasn't a countryman. Small boys in cities don't have much opportunity for tracking Red Indians. And as those odd little corners so accessible to the road are alive with courting couples' cars in the holiday season, he may well have thought a few more tyre marks would go unnoticed. As it would have done, had we no reason to believe foul play was involved.'

David said, 'We're sure he hoped you wouldn't, and only set up his alibi and Gordon Robertson as insurance policies.'

'Quite useful policies.' The Chief Constable took a typed sheet from his desk. 'He left his home in St Martin's at some period after receiving a phone call from Mr Smith at nine-thirty a.m. We've had reports of the Audi being seen leaving Midstreet shortly before ten a.m. and driving in the direction of the mainland. According to his statement, he drove into Astead intending to change three books at the public library, but had such difficulty trying to find a parking place as it was market day that after wasting roughly thirty minutes he changed his mind and drove straight over to Harbour. He stopped *en route* to make a phone call from the public box just over Coxden bridge. The manageress of the Tudor Rooms, Astead, recalls receiving a call from Mr Francis Denver just after eleven a.m. asking if his wife had arrived. She had not, and nor had she booked a table.' He glanced at me, but I said nothing. She was dead; Gordon had had it tough enough and so had the Smiths. 'H'mmm. Yes. Well, at eleven-thirty a.m. he met you both on Harbour Marsh and after a few minutes' conversation ran you back to the inn, drove on to Harbour, bought six gallons of petrol at Wattle's Garage and offered a lift to Cliffhill to Mrs Joan Burnham of 2 Harbour Cottages who gladly accepted as she had just missed the eleven-forty bus and knew him by sight. He left Harbour at about eleven-fifty a.m. and at that same time Mrs Doreen Burt of 9 Harbour Cottages told you that Mrs Francis Denver was waiting to speak to you on the telephone. And you took that call, Rose.' He lowered the paper. 'Two very useful witnesses for the defence, and particularly you, my dear. Susan's friend and neighbour who knew her voice. A theory can be correct, yet singularly hard to prove. Juries like first impressions. If this had come to court, I'm afraid a good defence lawyer would have made mince-meat out of you over this one.'

I sat straighter. 'Despite Mike Wattle's evidence? The

bits of mohair on that blue scarf? The fact that Lymchurch is twelve miles cross-marsh from Astead crossroad? That two separate members of the public have reported seeing a motor-cyclist in shiny black jacket, black skid-lid, with a black muffler round the lower half of his – or her – face haring to and from the crossroads and along part of the northern stretch of the Ditch road sometime just before and just after twelve? I know you haven't found that muffler yet and probably won't if the sea got it, but I'll bet it was Angie le Vere's, though I'm sure she didn't ring me from Astead crossroads. Like I've said, she wouldn't give me the number to ring her back even though she said she was short of change – and in a hurry. That, I believe. I don't think she rang from Lymchurch either. Too risky. Someone in the post office might've seen her after she bought the stomach tablets. I expect she stopped at one of the lonely boxes on the marsh. Much safer. And as for my first assuming it was Sue speaking – of course I did, even though, as I've said, something about that call worried me. But at the time I'd no reason to think it would be anyone but Sue.

'Yes,' I added, 'yes, I did then know Angie had been on the stage, and seemed a casual acquaintance of Francis. I'd no idea then they were having an affair, or that she could do such marvellous female impressions. I only discovered that when David triggered her into doing them at the party. Probably, if she hadn't had so much gin – and thought David equally tanked-up – she wouldn't have done them. She liked doing her party-piece and she didn't like me much. She had a good laugh doing me – did me wonderfully – but I'm sure it was later, when she'd sobered, that she realized she might've given me some nasty ideas and decided she'd better do something about me. She'd have guessed I told David, and heard from Francis that I'd told Mrs Smith and others, that Sue had rung me. So why not another sad accident. Huh!' I snorted. 'With every respect, Sir Norman, I'm almost sorry I can't ask the defence lawyer why a woman with nothing to hide who knew about guns should want to pull a Lüger on me. I don't know if juries have soft spots for widows, but I do wonder just how soft that spot would be if Angie and Francis were still alive and this had come to court. Attractive young widow – having it off with a younger man up to the day of her elderly husband's death and said younger man now on trial for murdering his wife. Blimey! The jury would gladly have crucified her! Juries come from the general public. In theory, the public drools with sympathy over widows. In practice, as most widows learn fast, especially if they're young, we get sorted into two types – the moaning and the merry. The public does its best to forget the former and think the worst of the latter.' I suddenly noticed David's grin and the Chief Constable's bemused expression. 'Sorry. Got carried away.'

'Not at all, my dear. Interesting. On second thoughts, I'm almost sorry you won't have to tackle the defence lawyer. I should've remembered you're your father's daughter. Rosser Endel,' he confided to David, 'was a delightful, easy-going chap – until he decided to do battle. In that event, all prudent chaps took to the hills.'

'I know just what you mean, sir.'

'Quite so. Well – yes – here we are twelve-twenty p.m. Denver dropped Mrs Burnham outside Findlay's Bank, Cliffhill, and kept his appointment with the manager, Mr Martin Geddes, and left at twelve-forty-five saying he intended to return by the mainland Cliffhill–Astead clearway to save time as he was due to meet Mr Smith at one-fifteen p.m. Twenty-seven miles by the clearway, thirty-one by the Ditch road. No reports of his car being seen on either road or until he arrived at Mr Smith's office just after one-fifteen. He remained in Mr Smith's presence until called to identify his wife's body at four p.m.' Sir Norman breathed heavily. 'Must admit, not much time.'

'Only needed a few minutes, sir. He'd a fast car and had picked his time well. Astead market day; Cliffhill Art Show day; harvesting, hedging and ditching and tourist season over; twelve to one, the agricultural dinner hour. I expect he had the Ditch road to himself and reached the hidden Allegro just before one p.m. He transferred the body, crashed the car in that sheltered sharp bend of the Ditch, thumped the tree, put the hat back on to remind any concerned that the kid had seen "the lady" wearing it, rolled the body into the water, nipped back to his Audi and on to Astead. All he had left to do was get rid of the rug and burn that fodder. Home and dry.'

'Perhaps he might've been,' I said, 'had he burnt it with the fodder.'

'Too risky, love. Burning wool makes smoke and smells foul. Safer to shove it down into a dyke well away from Midstreet and the Ditch.'

'I agree, Lofthouse. A dyke on Harbour Marsh must've seemed ideal with those sea outlets so close.' He sipped his drink and looked at us over the rim of the glass. 'You think he dealt with both the night of her death.'

'When he was being the bereaved husband with his phone off the hook and doors locked to all comers. Just in case anyone saw or heard him take his car out, when he rang Rose first thing next morning he told her he'd spent hours walking over the marsh. What more natural than that he should want to get off his home marsh haunted by thoughts of his wife? Probably he left the car a couple of miles from the inn and walked down. And got on with the job.'

'Singularly unfortunate for him that you chose to picnic on the beach next day – and fortunate for young Robertson. You don't require me to explain how our attention was drawn to him. Poor young Susan. A pretty, spoilt, brainless chatterbox. Disastrous combination. One can't wonder the husband knew precisely what was going was going on since her entire home village knew. She seems to have met him regularly at that particular place in the woods. We'd no alternative to asking Robertson a few questions, and once he appreciated the potential gravity of his situation, he was very honest with us. He said he had arranged to meet her there at ten-thirty the following morning on the previous evening when he drove her home from Cliffhill in the van he'd hired to take his pictures to the exhibition. Fortunately for him, he could only afford the van for that day. He couldn't conceal a body on his Norton. What confused the situation, until you provided the probable solution, was his insistence that later that same evening Susan rang his lodgings from, she said, her home, asking him to meet her at noon instead of earlier, and saying she would explain why when she saw him. He assumed her husband to be in her vicinity. But the next day, when Denver was asked what telephone calls from home his wife had made on the night in question, he insisted she had only made one to her mother and had not left the house again after her return from Cliffhill. Robertson was alone in his lodgings when the alleged call came through and we couldn't trace it now we've all gone automatic.'

'Hence Angie le Vere's mercy dash from Lymchurch.'

'Unproven, Rose, but, I suspect, correct.'

David sat up. 'Gordon didn't keep that date?'

'He did, but has insisted that as always he used the clear-way and entered the woods from the Astead side. He found no car awaiting and, according to his statement, he waited in the clearing for about thirty minutes, then returned to his lodgings by his habitual route, shut himself in his studio and got on with some picture. He became so engrossed he forgot the time and lunch until he belatedly remembered the exhibition and hurried to the town hall. Unfortunately for him, no one saw him during this period. In confidence,' he added, 'it was his forgetting his lunchtime beer that made it seem more probable that this account was true. I'm told the chap's a good artist. Kind of thing a good artist would do, unless he had a guilty conscience. If he had, I'd have expected him to need his beer and the alibi.'

I looked at David. 'You said that.'

'Is that so?' The Chief Constable looked at David. 'I'm informed Mrs le Vere's death was caused by the cumulative effects of sleeping pills taken after alcohol. You know, of course, that Dr McCabe found the bottle still two-thirds full under her pillows when he discovered she had died in her sleep yesterday morning. Doesn't look like suicide. Suicides more usually empty the bottle. It had only her fingerprints on it. Most correctly, Dr McCabe didn't touch it or allow anyone near the body until Harry Wattle got the message to us when he rowed you both to Harbour and our chaps managed to get down to the inn. From all the evidence we have, she died accidentally.' He paused. 'Do you both agree?'

We shook our heads and I left it to David. He was less likely to say too much. He said, 'Not that we think you'll ever be able to prove us right on this one.'

'Denver?'

'Yes.'

'When?'

'Probably, very shortly before Rose woke. We now think it was the sound of his going into six and getting down from the window that actually woke her. He was down when she spotted him and had obviously already decided the rug must be in Rose's room and how to clear the inn to give him the chance to get back for it.'

'Yes. Possibly. How'd he kill her?'

'Injection of barbiturate while she was asleep. Just a pin-prick and no bruising, as it didn't have to go into a vein. He could have had the opportunity then as she was sleeping alone in the McCabe's room. After her hysterics following the Lüger business, Nick and Linda McCabe had put her in Nick's bed, he'd given her a mild sedative, waited till she was asleep, then gone next door, got into Renny's bed and being so tired gone flat out. Linda stayed with Angie, but apparently, after lying there unable to sleep or stop thinking of Renny's death, she got very scared. Angie was deeply asleep, so the poor kid nipped next door and crawled in beside her husband without waking him. It was Rose backing out her car that woke him and he sent his wife back to Angie immediately and dashed in to look at her before he dashed on outside. Rose's car hadn't yet gone up, but Harry was shouting his head off. Angie slept through it all – and she would have, if Francis got in that shot. It wouldn't do the job for a few hours. He could've put that bottle under her pillow. God knows where he got it – probably out of her handbag as it had her name on it. He'd the nous to handle it with great care. Nick McCabe didn't know she had the stuff. I guess she got them quite legally from her family doctor – that wasn't Nick. Upset him badly. He hadn't thought of looking in her handbag, but after Renny died as she was in such a state he searched their room and locked in his medical bag every medicine he found.'

'So he told us. He gave it as his opinion that she must've woken while you were all occupied with the aftermath of the sea's incoming, but was too confused to be aware of what was happening and just stumbled out of bed for her pills, took the bottle back to bed, swallowed a few, went back to sleep and died without waking at around seven a.m., but this was not discovered until two hours later as the rest of you were all so tired that you slept late.'

David looked over his glasses at the Chief Constable. 'Nick McCabe could be right. We doubt it. That's all.'

'Not quite all. Why would Denver have wanted to kill her? Tired of her? Or to close her mouth? Or,' he suggested unemotionally, 'both?'

'Probably both.'

'Yes. Yes. Sufficient motives for a man who had already murdered once. How do you suggest he got hold of the barbiturate?'

'Bought it somewhere abroad on his business trips. Not all countries are as sticky about selling dangerous drugs over the counter as this one.'

'Possibly not, but how'd he have known it would serve his purpose and how to use it?'

I caught David's fleeting glance and the cue. 'I expect you know he was raised by an uncle after his parents' death, Sir Norman.'

He looked at me sharply. 'Gerald Smith told me some years ago. Died when Denver was at university leaving him without other relatives. I never heard the uncle's profession.' He frowned in quick comprehension. 'Medicine?'

'Yes. Not a GP, a specialist in toxicology. Different name as he was Francis's mother's only brother. Most kids pick up bits of information from their fathers' or guardians' jobs. Francis may even have inherited his textbooks. If not, he'd have known which books to look up.'

David added, 'And he was far too intelligent to pick the kind of obvious poison that could be traced. With sleeping pills that were barbiturates under her pillow, why should anyone stop to wonder why she had a high concentration of barbiturate in her blood at the post-mortem?'

'Why indeed?' The fine-boned, distinguished face set in hard lines. 'Very intelligent chap. Doing very well professionally, I'm informed.' He paused for thought, then went on, not inconsequentially, 'The freak wave that broke Harbour Wall was seen by a coastguard. Sixty foot high and an exceptionally high tide, he says. I'm glad it doesn't appear to have done the inn much damage. A nice old building. Empty of guests now?'

'Temporarily,' I said. 'The McCabes left this morning to stay with friends in London until the inquests. The East Anglian farmers have gone home and the Evans-Williamses have cancelled all bookings for the next two weeks. The cellar floors are still under water and the cold store's wrecked, but the ground floor and yard are drying out. They'd started working on the wall before we left today and already the old harbour was beginning to look like a lake. The swans were enjoying it. And the ducks.'

'Duck, my dear,' corrected the Chief Constable paternally, as if his mind were elsewhere. 'The birds won't enjoy their lake long. All the dyke pumps on the marsh are working overtime. They'll soon have that wall back in shape and Harbour Marsh back on the map – until the sea comes in again. It will. But whether that'll be in another century or two, or next month or next week, who can say? One can merely say the return is inevitable. Inevitable,' he repeated, 'as the probability that somewhere in this country at this moment some other over-patient husband or wife is approaching breaking point and contemplating murder as a solution. Yet divorce is so much easier now, and safer.'

'A divorce wouldn't have suited Denver, sir. This was her home territory. If he'd divorced her, even if he had insisted on staying in St Martin's – and he could've had a problem about the house as it was a joint wedding present and his father-in-law is a lawyer – but even if he stayed in another house, he'd have lost one hell of a lot of friends and influence. If you'll forgive my saying it – you marshfolk stick together more than most, specifically where incomers are concerned.'

'I fear we must accept that as fair comment, Rose. Go on, Lofthouse.'

'Denver liked life on the marsh. He liked the social scene, the social status he acquired when he married into an old, respected, comfortably affluent local family. I'll lay a year's pay he had hoped to get away with murder and continue living in St Martin's first as a sorrowing widower for a respectable period of mourning. And then' – David studied the lighted end of his cigarette – 'I guess he'd have looked around for another wife and picked one who could help him maintain his chosen image.'

The Chief Constable studied David's closed face. 'Were that event now possible,' he observed dryly, 'in my considered opinion the second Mrs Francis Denver would be ill-advised to insure her life in her husband's favour. However' – he rose – 'let us leave the subject and rejoin my wife, as I feel sure our dinner is waiting. . . .'

We were on the road to Endel in the elderly Cortina we had hired from Joe Wattle when I said abruptly, 'He must have known about the girl who slipped off Ben Gairlie.'

David was driving. 'Bound to. When the cops start digging the dirt they dig good.'

'Not good enough to turn up his uncle's job.'

'He died over fifteen years ago. They've not had time to dig that deep and don't have to now. But it's only just over four years back that the girl friend he'd been living with for a couple of years just happened to slip off a mountain path and fall to her death. No coroner's inquest involved as it happened in Scotland and the local Fiscal was satisfied it was an accident, but there'll be a record of it. Bound to have interested the local cops just as it did our Helen and our Johnnie, as it happened a few weeks after he first met Sue in Majorca. Just up for a nice long weekend in the

Highlands, she said, and walked up the mountain a little higher than was wise as it was such a lovely day and the poor girl slipped and was over before he could grab her. Tragic accident, the Fiscal said, and commended the gallant English lad for his bravery in climbing down and attempts to resuscitate her with the kiss of life. Yeuk bloody yeuk! Just a kid over from Ireland training as a nurse and one of a large family with nowt but her pay packet. Too bad, baby – nice knowing you. Shove off.'

I shuddered. 'My God. Must you?'

'Yep,' he snapped. 'I ain't his broken-hearted mixed up old man, nor his old man's doting childless wife. I don't buy that deprived upbringing excuses all codswollop. I grew up with too many kids who didn't know their fathers' names and have since made bloody good to spare one small tear for our Francis. Let's get off this road.'

He was silent till he took the next side turning off the main marsh road and drew up in a tractor entrance to a field. He switched off the engine. 'So his mother and Johnnie had it off but couldn't marry as she already had a hubby, but no other means of support, and Johnnie was a minor just out of school, dependent on parents who cut up nasty and packed him off to Canada for two years. Tough, yes. Not as tough as it could've been had his legal father not had the decency and generosity to play ball if only to spare his good name. He still played bloody ball and continued supporting a child he knew was not his after his wife died and up to his own death, when the wife's brother took over. The world's stiff with orphans who've been raised happily by uncles and aunts. Uncle must've been a charitable and broadminded bloke, or he'd not have told Francis the truth and allowed Johnnie access to his son. Uncle could have refused. He was the legal guardian, and natural fathers have no rights in law. Francis wasn't deprived of affection; he was bloody loaded with father-figures plus our Helen teetering around in the background longing to be a mum-figure as she couldn't have kids of her own. But I do believe her story about never feeling she could trust him even when he was a lad and what she said about Renny sharing this view. "Uncle Renny" to Francis when he was a kid. Christ. When poor old Uncle Renny walked in on Francis having that slop session with you, that signed his death warrant. Francis recognized him all right and though Renny had always kept his mouth shut for Johnnie's sake, even – I'll bet – to Angie, with Sue dead Francis was not taking chances on Renny's opening his mouth to you. I think Renny would've done just that, if he'd had time. He hadn't taken much of a shine to you until he realized you were a kid the same age as his daughters. He wouldn't want anyone to do dirt to them and he wasn't doing it to you. Sue plus girl friend dead. You just might be next on the list. He had to talk to you – only he never had time.' He slapped himself impatiently. 'Where in hell are my fags?'

I found the packet on the floor. 'Here.'

He grabbed it from me and in the lighter's flame I saw the anger in his face. I kept quiet as he hadn't finished and I had quite a few things on my mind.

He said, 'He no more gave a damn about rubbing out old Renny than when he risked rubbing out his old man with a load of shot just to keep him out of the road while you were around to minimize your chances of spotting the family resemblance. The Smiths and all their classy chums must never know the hideous truth. Very nice people, the Smiths. And Mr Smith is a lawyer. The less he heard about Francis's past, the better. No wonder the Evans-Williamses were so on edge when you first arrived, then being experienced hotel-keepers recognized they'd overdone the ice and fell over backwards with the big hallo. My turning up was a right bonus for them – and sonny's shotgun kindly handed them another. Why worry? Only winged. But I'll bet Harry caught on last year when Francis first made his play for Angie and breathed the word in Walt's ear. So Walt sent me horsing over and horsed over himself.'

I said absently. 'Walt likes Mr Smith a lot. Years ago when he was young and Walt's father died, Mr Smith managed to save Walt's mother and her five kids from being evicted from their tied cottage and got her the tenancy for life. She's still in it and Mr Smith still hasn't sent in his bill. Walt wouldn't tell me or anyone anything that might harm Mr Smith. I see now Walt was hinting that Francis might be out to get you. I knew what he meant but was too dumb to see who.'

'You weren't alone.' He took the subject back to Mrs Evans-Williams's confidences last night, and I thought of the relief she had tried so hard to keep battened down. 'Poor old Johnnie, broken-up as hell, blaming himself for everything and refusing to accept it was Francis who shot him.'

'He can't really believe that.'

'Don't be bloody dumb again! Of course not. His story and he's sticking to it like he's stuck to the story that he only insisted on moving from Cornwall to be nearer but not too near the boy. Never one word, she said, about feeling the need to keep an eye on him after the Scottish caper – just in case, she said – remember?'

I remembered. And something else she had said. ('Perhaps it wasn't his fault. Please, never breathe a word of this to Johnnie or anyone, but – well – there was bad blood on his mother's side. Her father was a drunkard and killed a man in a brawl and there was a terrible scandal and then he was put away as unfit to plead or something. It was all a long time ago, but I've always been sure that was why his uncle never married. He was a doctor. He knew about these things and it's no good pretending, blood is thicker than water and these – well – things – can be handed on to later generations.')

David was still talking : '. . . even if the brewer's offer was good, can't have been much fun at their age leaving their cosy pub, crossing the country and starting again from scratch. But Johnnie wanted to watch over the son he'd always longed for and she wanted what Johnnie wanted. And Francis knew they'd let him get away with one murder they couldn't prove, so why not use them again? Of course he pussy-footed in and out of the joint as he pleased. It bloody was his home from home.'

'As was Harbour Marsh. Which was why they didn't fancy the idea of my sitting around sketching.'

'Yep.'

We sat in silence for quite a while and listened to the croaking frogs, the slither of the slight wind in the dark rushes, the shrill scream of a hunted rabbit, the hoot of a solitary owl, the distant sighs of the sea, and our own thoughts.

'David.'

He didn't turn his face from the blackened windscreen. 'Yes?'

'I know what you've been saying, but why do you really think he killed Sue?'

'For the same reason he killed Angie and his former girl friend. Sue'd served her purpose and was dispensable.'

I breathed a little more easily, but still very carefully. 'Helen's right. Must be insanity in the family.'

'Balls. He wasn't insane. Just a cold-blooded killer.'

'Normal people aren't killers–'

'Never heard of wars, Rose? Or are you going to tell me every bloke who carries a gun for his country is a nutter?'

'That's totally different – '

'The only difference is that in war the killing's legalized. If there wasn't a streak of the killer in the normal male psyche, no government on earth would ever be able to raise an army. I'm not sure it's in the normal female psyche, as those who have the literal sweat of producing life are less likely to enjoy taking it. To kill is a male primitive instinct most of us manage to control if only for our own self-preservation. The law preserves us, so we preserve the law, unless we have the conceit to think we can beat it. He had. As for all that nice handy bad-blood eyewash – remember we got it from Helen who must've got it from Johnnie who almost certainly got it from his parents. Naturally, they'll have blamed the woman. Who in hell doesn't? And she was in her twenties and married and Johnnie was under age at a time when the conventions mattered a hellish lot more than now. They'll have slung every bit of mud they could scrape up at her. Maybe her dad was an alcoholic; maybe he did kill a bloke in a brawl. Or maybe dad had just had the odd one too many when a fight started up and he got in-volved and rather than face that scandal some smart lawyer managed to brush it under the carpet with an insanity plea – if that's what happened. How do we know it's true? How can anyone be sure of getting at the truth of a forty-year-old story handed on verbally and finally coming out of an openly hostile mouth third or fourth down the line?'

'I suppose you're right.'

He swung round to face me. 'You'd know I was bloody right if you'd stop thinking with your emotions and go back to using your brain. Francis used his but good. Every move, every word he said to you, carefully thought out. Remember what you told me about that slop session. Were those the words of a madman? Or the words of a very smart operator who knew just how deep to dig in the knife to get your empathy?'

I didn't answer until my mind had rerun that conversation. He sat still, not touching me, not even smoking. 'Yes. He had a good act. I'll say! No guy was ever more astounded than when I told him about your car – and there's a bit I haven't yet told you in here. He actually tried to blame you for that one.'

'Oh, aye?' There was an odd note in his tone. 'Why'd he think I'd done it?'

'To give you an excuse – no, alibi – he actually said. "alibi". God, am I dumb to have missed that Freudian slip till now. To give you an alibi for hanging around me.'

'Bright as they came, that lad.'

'What do you mean?'

'He got it in one.'

'*What*?' I was furious. 'Do you mean you –'

'Hell, love, I didn't intend the bloody job to blow up. I merely wanted to bugger up the engine a bit, (a) as he guessed, to give me a good excuse for hanging around a little longer to try and work out what, if anything, was going on, and (b), just in case that bathroom job had someone's name on it, to get in ahead before the next near-miss connected with the inn. Even the most superstitious start asking awkward questions about a fourth.' He laughed quietly. 'I sure buggered that one up. I didn't spot the petrol leak. I've told the insurance bloke I'm not claiming on it. This is why the replacement's taking longer. It ain't one. New sale.'

I was shaking my head slowly from side to side but that hadn't cleared it. 'You – you – buggered up your own engine to that extent? You? The wonder boy of BCC! Einstein junior? The eyes and ears of the county constabulary – joined the wrong wires?'

'That's right. Like old Walt said, when a lad's courting his mind's not where it should be.'

'My darling idiotic man' – I put a hand on his arm – 'you could've been burnt to death – '

'Like two nights back.' He caught my hand and held it between his own. 'Maybe,' he said softly in a voice he hadn't used for two nights, 'maybe you're right not to ask me to wed you, my love. If you want to make sure there's no daft blood in the family, don't hitch with Lofthouse. Hand him a screwdriver to fix up a neat wiring failure and he blows up his own car; show him a bit of vital evidence floating in with the tide and he closes his eyes for his afternoon nap; send him hot-foot after a killer and he forgets to take off his glasses though the night's dark as the inside of a cow's stomach and he can't see a bloody thing with them on.' He kissed my hand. 'Dead right, Rosie. You'd not want to hand on my blood to your kids. There's always the strong chance the little sods might take after dear old dad.'

I laid my free hand on his. 'So you know?'

'Now. I'd wondered sometimes while I was away. It could've been wishful thinking. It was last night that I caught on. I saw the expression in your lovely face when our Helen was going on about blood being thicker than water and uncle staying single. And why shouldn't he? Maybe he loved a married woman, or the girl he loved had died and he didn't fancy second-best, or maybe he fancied lads but being of his generation kept that to himself and made do with cold baths. But when I saw how you looked, I knew I'd wasted a lot of sweat over the way Francis looked at you down by the net-house. I saw then that, for all you'd said of his passionate devotion to Sue, he fancied you like the cat fancies the canary. If Renny reckoned Francis had your name next on the list, I think he was right – and your chum Sir Norman thinks the same though he doesn't know about Renny as we'd enough for him without that. I'll bet it crossed his mind, same as it did mine in the event, that Angie had a better motive than you put into words for pulling that Lüger on you. She knew enough about blokes to know Francis wasn't popping in on you to be neighbourly. You were younger, much prettier, and loaded. She was already in so deep over Sue that she'd not much to risk and one hell of a lot to gain if you met with another of those nasty fatal accidents.'

'That means you think Francis killed her – '

'Because you were next on the list? Maybe. And who was on the list after you? But on that one, Francis, Angie – the lot of us – were on to a dead duck. You weren't kidding when you said once was enough. But it was only last night I properly understood why. It's not the late Charles D. He's dead and gone – and so are all the Endels but you and that's the way you want to keep it. You've decided the Endel blood, like the entail, dies with you. After you, Lofthouse can have the lot even though he doesn't bloody rate it or want it. Just you, Rosie.' He hesitated, then went on unsteadily, 'You know I love you like hell and have since I first met you and you hated my guts. I know you don't hate them now and haven't for years. Up to the other night I just thought you liked me. After that – and last night – I've been wondering – am I another reason for your determination to stay a widow? Or is that just more wishful thinking?'

'No.'

His hands gripped mine and for about a minute we just looked at each other in the darkness. Then I had to say it. 'I love you, David. I'd love to marry you, but I won't. It wouldn't work. Dirty tricks don't. I'll never risk handing on my Endel blood and you know exactly why. You may say now you don't give a damn if we never have kids, but you will, duckie, you will. You'll probably want to clout me for this, but family man is written all over you.'

'Oh, aye? Thanks for spelling it out and – just thanks so bloody much – ' He pulled off his glasses, pulled me into his arms and kissed me as if for the first time. 'I'll say this for you, love,' he muttered, 'whatever you are, life isn't dull when you're around – and when you're not around it isn't life – just existence.'

Later, he said, 'Dirty trick, eh? Family man, am I? Like they say, you learn something new every day. This lot needs sorting out, but not tonight as I'm too bloody happy to think straight. Tell you what. Once this Harbour business is all cleared up, why don't we get right away from the marsh on our own? There must be some place somewhere where we'll have the time to give time to our own problems. Will you come with me?'

'Just good friends on a jolly spree?'

'What else? Seeing you're still determined not to make an honest man of me. Deal? Right. That's settled then. Time we made tracks for Endel. I don't know about you, love, but this return to the British way of life has aged me fast and I'm more than ready for my bed.'